MARRIED BY SCANDAL

ARRANGED MARRIAGES OF THE FAE

TESSONJA ODETTE

Married by Scandal

TESSONJA ODETTE

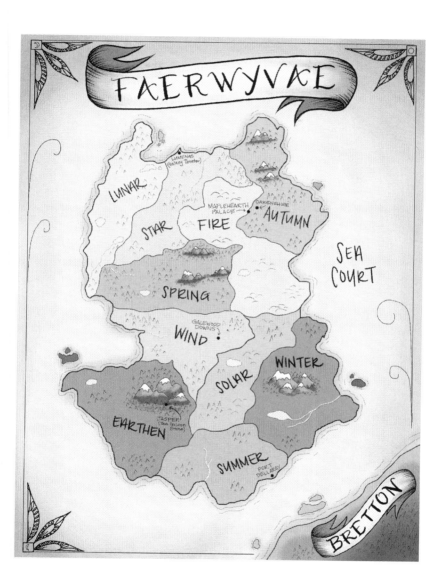

1

The first man I loved died in my arms. I grieved as I watched him take his last breath, my tears mingling with his blood. Time seemed to stand still, even as the battlefield around us continued to roar with explosives, shrapnel, and gunfire. He wasn't the first casualty of the war that raged over the isle of Faerwyvae twenty-two years ago, nor was he the last. But his death is the one I remember most, for my grief was an endless sea so vast I can still feel its echo. My tears so violent they could have flooded the world. The only thing stronger than my tears and sorrow was the heat of my rage.

Rage that his death hadn't been dealt by my own hand.

It wasn't the loss of him I lamented but the loss of my vengeance. He may have been my first love, but I didn't love him when he died. No, the wicked fae prince who'd twisted my mind with lust, lies, and manipulation had no place in my heart anymore. As I wept over his fallen corpse, I promised never, *ever* to be so foolish as to fall in love again.

I've kept that promise. Not once have I strayed from my convictions. Not once have I allowed myself to so much as fancy another man, aside from the occasional emotionless tryst. *Love* is a word that no longer exists in my vocabulary, alongside *lust* and *trust*.

Which is why the black-and-white photograph plastered over the front page of the scandal sheets is the most ludicrous thing I've ever had the displeasure to see. I stare down at my own likeness captured in what looks like a heated embrace with a middle-aged gentleman dressed in only his undergarments. The man's face is mere inches from mine, my mouth forming a soft *O*. What the photograph fails to express is that my lips weren't puckered in anticipation of a kiss but a shout of alarm. And I hadn't been melting into the embrace but frozen in shock over receiving such an unwanted advance.

My cheeks burn with the heat of my ire as I lift my eyes to the headline above the photograph, taunting me with its bold capital letters.

AMELIE   FAIRFIELD: BRILLIANT   FASHION DESIGNER OR HOMEWRECKING HARLOT?

With a groan, I crinkle the paper until it forms a tight ball in my fist. "To hell with the *Trundale Tattler*," I say.

Foxglove gives me a pitying look behind his horn-rimmed spectacles. The stout fae male would look quite sharp in his burgundy three-piece suit and gold cravat if it weren't for how aggressively he wrings his hands. "It's not...well, there's a chance no one will believe a word the paper says. The *Trundale Tattler* is renowned for its sensational and oftentimes incorrect gossip. You...you might not have a thing to worry about."

I huff a humorless laugh. "My dear Foxglove, the fact that you had to pause twice to organize your words tells me you hardly believe them yourself."

He gives me a guilty grin that might as well be a grimace. He knows I'm right. Foxglove is a pureblood fae —as evidenced by his pointed ears—which means he can't lie. Unlike myself. I'm only a quarter fae, giving me rounded ears and the convenient ability to lie just fine. Not that truths or lies help my situation right now. The damage to my reputation has already been done. Not to mention my career.

"It's not just the *Trundale Tattler* I have to worry about," I say. "This is the fifth scandal sheet I've graced this week alone. Every city I've been to has this damn photograph plastered to its front page. As of today, I've lost three clients, all married human women who would rather not invite a homewrecker into their house when they can get a custom gown from a more *appropriate* source."

My cheeks burn with indignation. How can I prove I didn't want Mr. Vance to try and kiss me? How can I express how repulsed I was to be propositioned by a married man? And why...*why* the bloody oak and ivy did it have to be the husband of my most elite human client? The Vance family is amongst the upper echelon of human aristocracy. If they shun me, others will follow. Never mind that the patriarch of said highly respected family is a complete and utter lecher. Why am I the one getting blamed for that son-of-a-harpy's depravity?

I squeeze the crumpled paper tighter in my palm and

toss it into the waste bin next to my table. It bounces off the mountain of discarded design sketches already spilling over the brim and lands by my foot. I glare down at it and kick it across the room with the toe of my silk shoe.

"You should really hire a maid, Amelie," Foxglove says, frowning at the mess my living room has become. It isn't just the waste bin that's cluttered. My whole cottage is in a state of disarray, with bolts of fabric lying over every surface, from the divan and tea table to the wing-back chair that stands askew beside my stone hearth. Sketchbooks litter my wooden table while dress forms stalk the far wall like silent, judging spectators.

What he doesn't realize is I like my cottage cluttered. It reminds me of the home I grew up in. My mother was an apothecary, and her shop was attached to our living quarters. While her shop was neat and organized, her work spilled into other areas of the house. The kitchen, in particular. I loved the sight of bundled herbs hanging from the ceiling, every shelf crammed with jars, dried botanicals, and other essential ingredients for Mother's tisanes, tinctures, and tonics. She wasn't nearly as messy as I am, but there's a comfort in my mess that my guests don't understand. With the afternoon light streaming through my windows, bringing with it a red-orange glow courtesy of the forever-fall leaves the Autumn Court is famous for, it makes my disarray look downright enchanting.

Besides, what use is there hiring a maid when my career might be at an end?

Throwing my head back, I release a tired groan. "Why did this have to happen? I miss the days when one's portrait could only be captured by hand. At least then one could easily question the validity of the sketches presented in the broadsheets. These cameras and flash bulbs are a nuisance."

Foxglove snorts a laugh.

I do the same. "I'm showing my true age, aren't I?"

"Darling, you don't look a day over twenty."

"Why, thank you," I say, giving an exaggerated flip of my copper hair. My enthusiasm over the compliment is feigned. Due to my fae heritage, I stopped aging in my twenties. I'm forty-two now, and sometimes I feel it. Other times, I'm struck with a sudden panic over the realization that aging has lost all meaning to me. Foxglove wouldn't understand the existential crisis I sometimes feel. He's a few hundred years old yet looks the same age as me. But he expected eternal youth his entire life, while I grew up thinking I was human.

"This will cheer you up," he says, reaching into the pocket of his waistcoat and extracting a folded strip of lace. He hands it to me with a grin.

As soon as the lace touches my palm, I'm entranced. It's woven from an impossibly delicate material, even finer and stronger than spider silk. The intricate pattern displays the most stunning detail. It puts the cream lace day dress I'm wearing to shame, even with the velvet ribbons and seed pearl embellishments I've added to the high collar and leg-of-mutton sleeves. The lace I'm holding now stands on its own as a work of art. I inspect every inch of the fabric, my previous worries forgotten. I know it's a temporary distraction, but it's one I'll take.

"What kind of silk was this made from?" I ask, lifting

my eyes from the lace to catch Foxglove's smug expression.

He waggles his brows, making his spectacles bounce on his nose. "Dragon silk."

My mouth falls open. "Dragon silk? That exists?"

"It does now. There's a rare breed of silk dragon that normally lives in the northern forests of the Spring Court. They weave their nests from the silk to keep their hatchlings warm. One of these dragons has decided to enter seelie society with her children and has taken up spinning silk."

I pull my head back in surprise. It isn't every day a rare unseelie creature joins society. Faerwyvae may be an isle inhabited by humans and fae in equal measure, but there remains some divide between the two people. Additionally, there exists two kinds of fae that don't always interact: the seelie and unseelie fae. Before humans came to the isle, all fae were unseelie— creatures, animals, and spirits. It wasn't until just over a thousand years ago, when the first humans inhabited Faerwyvae, that the fae learned to take on a secondary manifestation—seelie form, modeled after human likeness. But just because the fae *can* shift forms doesn't mean all of them *do*. In fact, some are firmly against it. The rarest types of fae often remain in their unseelie forms their whole lives, hiding out in the wild mountains and forests, far from society's influence. This is certainly the first time a silk dragon has come out to society amongst the humans and seelie fae. I've never even heard of such a creature before now.

"You can imagine how rare such silk has become," Foxglove says, a conspiratorial lilt to his tone. "With only one silk dragon producing such thread, it's an extreme luxury. Lucky is the person who can secure such a contract, am I right?"

I quirk a brow. "Let me guess. *You* are that lucky person?"

"Indeed, I am."

My shoulders slump. "Please don't tell me you're using dragon silk lace for doilies."

He lets out an affronted gasp, stuttering before he answers. "N-no. Of course not. I've learned my lesson about doilies, Amelie. I admit you and your sister were right about me going perhaps a tiny bit overboard with them."

I chuckle. That's the first time in over twenty years I've gotten him to admit to such a thing. After the war, Foxglove left his occupation as a royal ambassador to start a career in interior design. While his eye for fae design has always been phenomenal, he's had much to learn when it comes to designing interiors meant for humans. His first attempt was a parlor for my sister, the Unseelie Queen of the Fire Court. The room was so amusingly hideous, she had it replicated when she and her husband relocated to their current palace.

He gives a derisive snort. "I'll have you know, I'm making curtains with the lace, not doilies. Besides, I wouldn't poke fun if I were you. Not if you want me to share the benefits of such a prestigious contract."

I press the lace to my heart. "Do you mean it?"

"Of course I do," he says with a lighthearted roll of his eyes. "It would only make sense, considering we practically work together."

We don't so much work together as share a two-story design studio in the nearby city of Hawthorn. There we partner with our design teams to bring our respective creations to life.

"Although," Foxglove says under his breath, "one wouldn't know you had a separate workspace if they saw your living room."

I ignore his gibe and bounce on the balls of my feet. "Can I have this piece, then?"

"That's why I brought it." He gives a flippant wave of his hand, but I can tell he's pleased by my excitement.

With a squeal, I weave between my cluttered tables to the dress form standing in the shade between two windows. Upon it hangs an in-progress ballgown in a dusty rose brocade. The skirt falls in billowing layers while the back features a bustle and flowing train. The bodice is fitted with a ruffled off-the-shoulder neckline trimmed with lace. I've been staring at the gown for days, not fully satisfied with any of the lace I've attempted to use thus far. But this delicate fabric in my hand will be perfect.

With my tongue perched at the corner of my mouth, I get to work removing the pins securing the current lace trim to the dress. Then I replace it with the dragon silk lace, carefully pinning the fabric in place where I'll eventually sew it. It's just enough to fully finish the neckline, leaving me only a spare scrap to fold into a lace floret to adorn the center of the décolletage.

Finished, I step back to admire my work. "It's perfect." I bat my lashes at Foxglove in hopeful pleading. "Please tell me you have more to spare. I must trim the skirt with this too."

"I'll give you ten yards for now," he says, "but it's at the studio."

I reach for his hand and give it a squeeze. "Foxglove, you're a hero."

"Stop, you'll make me blush."

I turn back to the dress, but as I assess the gown once more, my bright mood dims. This ballgown was meant to grace the stage at Bartleby's next fashion showcase. Bartleby's is a department store famous for ready-to-wear apparel. It's a trend that began in the country of Bretton and made its way here about a decade ago. Other department stores have followed suit, but Bartleby's remains the premier establishment, specializing in high fashion at a reasonable price, without the long wait custom clothing requires. Furthermore, they cater to human clientele and take pride in showcasing ensembles made with human sensibilities in mind. Unlike popular fae fashions, which discarded corsets, undergarments, and weighty fabrics ages ago, human fashion continues to favor cinched waistlines, gravity-defying bosoms, and time-honored fabrics and silhouettes.

I've been learning the trade of dressmaking and design for over twenty years, but my career didn't take off until about five years ago. Ever since, most of my clients have been fae. I only recently snagged human interest, and for the first time, my work caught the eye of Bartleby's. I was invited to display my designs at the next four fashion showcases, the first having taken place last week. But my spring line never made it to the showcase stage. Because that was when Mr. Vance ruined everything.

Foxglove comes up beside me and wrings his hands. "Perhaps Evie can help."

I purse my lips. "I don't want my sister's help."

"But she would be happy to. You know that, right?"

I do, but I don't admit it out loud. The truth is, Evie would be eager to get me out of this mess. That's exactly why I can't let her. I already owe enough of my success to her. Being the sister of the infamous human-fae queen who helped lead the fae to victory in the war has provided me with easy renown amongst my fae clients. But the career I'm building with the humans...that's *mine* and I want to keep it that way.

I nibble my lip. "I'd prefer Evie didn't find out about this at all."

Foxglove gives me another one of his grimace-grins.

The blood leaves my face. "She already knows?"

"Fehr told me."

Fehr is Foxglove's husband, a djinn who serves my sister as her ambassador, Captain of the Guard, and... well, he's pretty much the head of everything at Maple-hearth Palace. I'm not surprised Fehr told Foxglove, but I'm starting to suspect Foxglove had more than lace on his mind when he paid me a visit.

"I promised Fehr I'd pass on a message from Evie," he says, tone brimming with apology. "The queen would like to have a word. She says it's urgent."

2

My stomach is a ball of knots as I walk through the woods toward my sister's palace. It isn't a far walk, as my cottage is located in the forest just outside the royal grounds, but each step feels too long. Or too short, perhaps. All I know is I dread what this meeting will bring. I know it's about the scandal, but...what about it is so urgent?

Evie won't be upset. She'll be supportive, I'm sure. She always is. To be honest, I have no reason to be nervous around my sister at all. There was a short time, decades ago, when our relationship was wrought with mistrust and anger, but things changed. She forgave me for my mistakes, and I forgave her for hers. Nonetheless, I hate causing trouble for her. It reminds me too much of the greatest trouble I ever caused. Trouble that led to war.

I almost wish Foxglove had come with me, but he mumbled something about needing to return to the studio and then bid me a hasty farewell. His sudden fretfulness told me he might have more insight into my imminent conversation than he let on.

The bright fall trees begin to thin, giving me my first glimpse of Maplehearth Palace. It's always a breathtaking sight, with half the sprawling structure nestled in the Autumn Court woods, the other half perched before sandy dunes and rolling golden mountains. The palace was built on the border between the Autumn and Fire Courts, to provide my sister and her husband—King Aspen, the Unseelie King of Autumn—a shared residence where they could rule over their respective courts side by side. Visually, the transition from one court to the other is seamless. The leaves of the trees on this side of the border glow brighter the closer they are to the Fire Court, making their red leaves reminiscent of flames. The dunes on the opposite side shift from gold to a more muted brown, resembling tree trunks and soil before giving way to Autumn entirely. The weather too shifts incrementally. Every step I take toward the palace gate brings warmer air. I know if I cross over to the Fire Court side it will feel stifling.

Despite being of fire fae blood like my sister, I don't have nearly the same tolerance for heat. Which is why I chose to locate my cottage in Autumn, a court that suits the element of fire well enough with its red, orange, and gold leaves. During sunset, the sky lights up like a glowing inferno.

I approach the palace gate on the Autumn Court side, and the weather warms to a mild summer climate. Despite the growing heat, I resist removing my coat, knowing it will be much cooler once I step inside the palace. Plus, it's my favorite coat, one made of chartreuse brocade. Not only is it stunning, but I like to think it brings out the green of my eyes. The thought sends my gut roiling, reminding me of what Mr. Vance had said before he embraced me.

Your eyes are so beautiful, Miss Fairfield. They're swimming with love. I can see you feel the same as I do.

What a fool! My eyes haven't swum with love in over twenty years, and if they were ever to do so again, it would be over a fine garment, not a man.

I march the remaining few steps to the palace gate, each stomp expressing my rage. When I tell the guard I'm expected by my sister, my tone comes out far more demanding than I intend. At least anger feels better than dread.

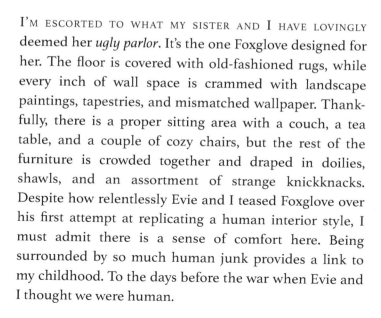

I'M ESCORTED TO WHAT MY SISTER AND I HAVE LOVINGLY deemed her *ugly parlor*. It's the one Foxglove designed for her. The floor is covered with old-fashioned rugs, while every inch of wall space is crammed with landscape paintings, tapestries, and mismatched wallpaper. Thankfully, there is a proper sitting area with a couch, a tea table, and a couple of cozy chairs, but the rest of the furniture is crowded together and draped in doilies, shawls, and an assortment of strange knickknacks. Despite how relentlessly Evie and I teased Foxglove over his first attempt at replicating a human interior style, I must admit there is a sense of comfort here. Being surrounded by so much human junk provides a link to my childhood. To the days before the war when Evie and I thought we were human.

I plant myself on the couch, not bothering to adopt any sort of ladylike posture, and instead slump against the cushions. A few moments later, Evie enters the room. As soon as I see what she's wearing, I release a groan.

My sister closes the door behind her and pauses. Her cheeks redden when she sees me frowning at her. "What?"

I gesture at the dress she wears, although the term *dress* is generous. It's nothing more than a long swath of red chiffon draped and secured with lazy ties and sad stitches. "Please tell me this is the only gown you've kept of the old ones I made for you."

She rolls her blue eyes and settles onto the couch next to me. "I kept them all, and I don't see why that should offend you."

"No, Evie, they're so ugly. I hardly knew what I was doing back then. Just look! Your hem is fraying."

She kicks off her low-heeled satin shoes and removes pins from her hair until her dark auburn strands fall around her shoulders. Then she mirrors my posture, slouching into the pillows at the other end of the couch, and throws her legs over mine. It's how we used to sit when we were little. The older we get and the less we age, the more we seek comfort in the past. Even though Evie stopped aging at the same time I did, she'll always be my little sister.

"I think these old dresses are comfortable," she says, smoothing out her crooked skirts.

"Yes, well, don't you dare wear those hideous old things where anyone important can see you."

She gives me a pointed look. "I practically came to power outfitted in these *hideous old things*."

She's right. When she first became Unseelie Queen of Fire—the very first part-human monarch to rule over a fae court—she did so in my designs, flaunting them as if they were the finest fashions the world had ever seen. I might have thought so too, back then. But now...

"Let me alter them at least," I say, tone pleading. "I'll return them to you far prettier than they are now."

With a laugh, she nudges me in the hip with her bare toe. "No, you're not taking my cozies. Besides, you're your harshest critic, Amelie. To your fans, these old things are probably worth a fortune."

My heart sinks at the mention of my fans. I can't help but be reminded of the handful of human clients who no longer consider themselves as such.

Evie must read the shift on my face, for her lips pull into a grimace. Angling her body to face me head on, she says, "We should talk about the scandal."

"Scandal?" comes an airy voice. A tiny feminine form encased in deep red flame floats over to the couch and perches on the backrest. It's Breeda, a fire sprite and one of my sister's most loyal companions. She props her chin in her dainty hands and pins me with a longing look. "I do so very much enjoy a good scandal. Please tell me it was a love scandal, Most Beautiful and Talented Amelie."

I snort a laugh at her version of a royal title. She often refers to my sister as Her Most Beautiful and Glorious Majesty, or something along those lines. "Hardly. There wasn't an ounce of love involved in this scandal."

"How did it happen, anyway?" Evie asks.

My eyes go unfocused as I force myself to relive that horrid event. "It was during Bartleby's showcase last week. I was set to present my line at noon, so I had some time to spare. Lydia Mangrove thought it prudent to fill my time with the offer of a new client." My tone turns bitter as I mention the last part. I never considered Lydia Mangrove to be my rival, but I do now. She's a half-fae fashion designer looking to break into the human market, just like me. I thought we were kindred spirits with the potential to become friends. I was wrong.

"I didn't know at the time," I say, "but Lydia had lost her account with the Vance family just before I secured the contract as Mrs. Vance's primary designer. So I didn't think anything of it when she told me Mr. Vance was seeking to have a suit made in the fae style for an upcoming event. She said he was in attendance and wanted me to take his measurements at once. I figured it would be brilliant to secure the favor of both Vances, so I approached him and brought him backstage into a changing room."

"Oh no," Evie says. I'm sure it isn't hard for her to guess where my story is going.

"Oh no, indeed. Stupidly, all matters of propriety fled my mind and I had him strip down for his measurements. That's when he declared his undying affection, said he's been yearning for me since the first day I stepped foot into the Vance home. Then he tried to kiss me. Which is, of course, the exact moment Lydia Mangrove pulled aside the curtain of the dressing room, providing a perfect view for the reporter and photographer she'd dragged along."

Evie's mouth falls open. "You were set up! I'm willing to bet Lydia Mangrove was let go by the Vances due to Mr. Vance's bad behavior and wanted you to suffer the same fate for replacing her."

"What a dirty harpy," Breeda says, her tone more fascinated than indignant.

I shrug. "It was my own damn fault."

"No, Amelie," Evie says. "How could you have known better? You've been working primarily with fae clientele since your career began. Fae aren't nearly as concerned as humans are over matters of propriety."

"That may be true, and I may not be guilty of what the scandal sheets insist, but my own naïveté is to blame."

Evie doesn't bother contradicting me. She knows I'm right. I was never the best at detecting ulterior motives.

"Besides," I say, "if I want to make a name for myself in the human world of fashion, I need to remember how to play by their rules. Taking a married man into a dressing room at a public event and asking him to strip down was an obvious line I should have known better than to cross."

"You didn't ask him to kiss you. That wasn't your fault."

Her words ease some of the tension in my chest. "No, you're right."

Breeda sprawls out on her belly, a wry grin on her tiny lips. "If anyone is to blame, it's Miss Most Idiotic and Rude Lydia Mangrove. Would you like me to pay her a visit? I'll sneak into her studio and burn her clothes to cinders if you think that would help." She says it in all innocence, batting her fiery lashes, but I have no doubt she means it. The fire sprite is full fae, which means she can't lie.

I release a sigh. "As much as I'd like to fantasize about getting revenge on Miss Mangrove, doing so won't help. My standing with Bartleby's has been compromised. If I do anything else to fan the flames of this scandal, my chance with the department store could be irrevocably ruined."

Breeda kicks her legs leisurely behind her. "If you change your mind, just ask. Or give me a signal. A wink, perhaps. No, a secret code word. I've got it! Just say *it's a good day for a heatwave*. I'll know what you mean."

I chuckle at the fire sprite's offer, but my sister's countenance remains stoic, brow furrowed. "Why is the opportunity with Bartleby's so important?"

"You know why," I say. "It could grow my career."

"What I mean is...why are you so determined to garner human validation? You're famous amongst the fae."

I hesitate before answering. I don't want to tell her that part of the reason is because the human side of my career is mine alone, unlike the fae side. She'd only feel guilty if she knew I harbored a smidge of resentment over the fact that my fame was spawned by my relation to *her*.

Instead, I offer a safer truth. "We may be part fae, but we're human too. I want to honor both sides of our heritage. There's a part of me that will always yearn for what we had when Mother was still alive."

A lump forms in my throat at the mention of Mother —Maven Fairfield, the most heartbreaking casualty of the war. She was executed by humans for treason, and I wasn't even there when she died. Instead, I was being manipulated and held captive by the man I thought I loved.

Evie's lips turn down as she fiddles with the fraying hem of her skirt. Breeda, on the other hand, seems to have grown bored with our dreary topic and has drifted over to my armrest, where she tiptoes back and forth like a ballerina.

"Anyhow," I say with forced nonchalance, "that's the story. Now...why did you want to talk to me about it? Foxglove said it was urgent."

She meets my eyes and chews a corner of her lip before answering. That's how I know I won't like what she's about to say. "I think I can help."

I hold up a hand. "I appreciate you wanting to help, but you can't save me from this. If you use your title to force Bartleby's to invite me back for the next showcase, it will only sow discord."

"That's not what I had in mind," Evie says, sitting straighter. "Instead, you're going to gain human favor and respect all on your own. Or...sort of on your own."

"What do you mean?" The dread forming in my gut makes me wonder if I'm better off not hearing her answer.

Her lips pull into a grimace. "How do you feel about marrying a human prince?"

3

Breeda clasps her hands to her chest and floats up next to my head. The red flames dancing over her minuscule body begin to flutter faster. "A prince? Oh, how completely and totally dreamy. You should marry him, Amelie."

"I don't even know who this prince is," I say, too stunned to take my eyes off my sister. "What are you talking about, Evie?"

"Do you remember the offer you made me a long time ago?"

"Define a long time ago," I say, although I have a sneaking suspicion I know exactly when—and what—she's referring to.

"Soon after the war, you said if I ever needed to arrange a marriage for political advantage, you'd marry anyone."

I wince. I had made such an offer, but not out of enthusiasm. It was more out of...resignation. Apathy. Which is a funny thing, considering only a few months before that, I'd have given anything for a favorable marriage. In fact, I *did* give everything for exactly that. And it blew up in my face. In everyone's faces.

"I remember," I grudgingly confess.

"Well, I've received a proposal from King Grigory."

My stomach lurches. King Grigory is the ruling monarch of Bretton, the very man who sought to annihilate all life on the isle during the war. Not just fae lives. The humans living here would have perished too, were it not for my sister and her allies. "I'm not marrying King Grigory. I may be forty-two, but he must be...at least a few decades my senior."

Breeda nods at Evie. "That is gross, Your Most Gracious and Beautiful Majesty. Don't we hate him?"

She gives Breeda a wry look, then turns the same expression to me. "I know better than to pair you off with that slimy bastard."

"Then...who?"

"One of his middle sons," she says, forcing a hopeful smile. "Prince Albert."

I blink at her a few times. "Prince Albert? You mean the entitled drunken rogue?" We don't get much news from Bretton, since we aren't exactly on good terms with the country we once went to war with, but I've heard enough about Prince Albert to form a solid opinion that he's nothing but a rake.

"Don't take this the wrong way," Evie says with a placating gesture, "but this might not be the best time to judge someone based on how they're presented in the scandal sheets."

I bite back the flurry of arguments burning my tongue. She has a point.

Breeda floats back to the top of the couch and perches on the backrest. "He's not old and gross, is he?"

"He's eight-and-twenty," Evie says.

Breeda gasps. "Ooh, a younger man."

Evie scoots closer to me. "King Grigory presented the Alpha Council with a marriage alliance as an act of goodwill to open talks on improving trade between our countries. By sending his son to establish a political marriage, we essentially possess a hostage."

I must admit, I can see the wisdom there. After the war, we closed off trade with Bretton. Most imports and exports go through Isola and other countries, which makes anything moving between Faerwyvae and Bretton rather expensive. Giving us a valuable hostage is a good way to ensure peace continues between our countries. And if Grigory isn't asking for a hostage in return, we hold the upper hand.

We already do, in truth. Even if Bretton were to resort to war with us, they wouldn't get far. Our victory ended when Fehr—Foxglove's djinn husband—helped forge a magic-infused barrier around Faerwyvae. It prevents humans from leaving or entering the isle without a pureblood fae escort. Additionally, the magic forms an invisible dome that protects Faerwyvae from any sort of attack, whether by land, sea, or sky. Although, with Bretton's rumored advancements in firearms and explosives, I'd hate to see our barrier's limits tested. Perhaps it's time we solidified a formal pact with Bretton.

Evie reaches over and places a hand on my shoulder. "What do you think, Ami?"

Her use of my childhood nickname has my heart softening. She's buttering me up like a scone. Still, I'm not sure how to answer.

This isn't the first time I've been offered an arranged marriage. Although *forced into* might be a better term than *offered*. Before the war, half the isle was claimed by humans under Brettonish rule, and peace was maintained with a treaty. According to it, two human girls were given as brides to the fae every hundred years. The event was called the Reaping, and during the last one, Evie and I were chosen to wed a pair of royal fae brothers. Being the eldest, I was engaged to the older brother, King Aspen, while Evie was paired with the younger, Prince Cobalt.

Not yet aware of our own fae heritage, neither of us were thrilled with the arrangement. I, however, adapted much faster than my sister. I was fascinated by our new environment, by the beauty and luster all around us, by the strange and gorgeous fashions. There was only one thing I couldn't resign myself to—marrying King Aspen. Instead of falling for my betrothed, I lusted after my sister's fiancé. Prince Cobalt seemed to share my feelings and offered me a happily ever after. I was so enamored with him that I failed to see his manipulations. I agreed to do anything he told me to if it meant we could be together. He formed a plan, and I went along with it without question. It wasn't until he began using fae compulsion on me and forced me to do unthinkable things that I realized the truth. By then it was too late. Cobalt had everything in place to steal the throne from his brother. There was nothing I could do about it. I could only follow the orders given to me under the influence of Cobalt's compulsion. Thus began the war.

My only solace is that my memories from that time are hazy. I vaguely recall the blood on my hands, the lives I took, the people I was forced to hurt.

But I'll never forget how much I hurt Evie. Everything I did with Cobalt was a betrayal against her, even if I didn't know it at the time. Even if I was powerless to change my actions after I discovered the truth.

Eventually, I broke free from the bonds of compulsion and joined my sister. She didn't trust me, and for good reason. But after Cobalt died, she finally understood. Understood that I was no longer the simpering, lustful girl that would risk everything for romance. That was why I told Evie she could marry me off. I figured it didn't matter if I was ever forced to wed. Love was meaningless, and I'd do anything for my sister's reign.

But that was then, and this is now. I've moved beyond resignation and apathy. Beyond the rage I felt following the death of my devious first love. Where a political marriage once seemed like something I could bear with numb tolerance if it helped Evie, it now feels smothering. Repulsive.

"I know you made that offer long ago," Evie says, tone gentle, "and I understand if you'd like to revoke it. I won't force you into an arranged marriage, but if you willingly agree, I think it could help you."

"How so?"

Her expression turns sly, calculating. It's a face I've seen many times before. "First of all, marrying a prince —a *human* prince—will automatically improve your reputation where this scandal is concerned. Not only will you gain the humans' respect by marrying such an important man, but it will also prove you aren't trying to steal your clients' husbands. Who would go after a humdrum married mortal when they have a prince at home?"

"No one," Breeda says, tone perfectly austere.

My sister's theory is sound. Human royalty is a novel concept in Faerwyvae. Following the war, the fae seized political control over the isle, reclaiming the land that was rightfully theirs to begin with. Humans were forbidden from reigning henceforth. These days, some fae royals have human or part-human partners, but no pureblood human is allowed to rule over any of the courts alone. So it makes sense that the humans would admire a Brettonish prince.

"Why me?" I ask, and it's a legitimate question. I couldn't have been the Alpha Council's first choice. The council is comprised of every ruler in each of Faerwyvae's eleven courts. With both a seelie and unseelie monarch in each court, that makes twenty-two royals. Of all the possible brides that could have been selected from their pool of respectable relations, I highly doubt I made the top of the list. Not even Evie's.

"To be honest," she says, "we've been working on this for a long time. We'd already chosen a bride, scheduled Albert's arrival and wedding date, but the bride decided to elope last minute."

"Was she that desperate to evade the marriage?"

"Perhaps. What matters to the council is finding a replacement and securing formal peace with Bretton. If we offer King Grigory the same terms and the same time-line, I don't think he'll mind his son having a change of bride. So long as she's a close relative to one of the royals —or a royal herself—the match will be adequate."

I huff a laugh. "I doubt Prince Albert will consider someone embroiled in scandal to be at all adequate."

"He won't be aware of your scandal. You know how slowly gossip travels between our two countries. Albert is scheduled to arrive here in one week, and the wedding is to take place at the end of the month, which is two-and-a-half weeks after his ship docks."

My heart leaps into my throat. I'd have to wed a stranger in just over *three weeks*?

Evie continues, oblivious to my moment of panic. "As soon as word goes around that you're engaged to a prince, all talk of that scandal will die out. By the time he's here, it will be like it never happened."

I find myself leaning toward my sister, drawn in by her logic. "But...but what if the people see through my ruse? What if they know the marriage is one of convenience, manufactured to clear my name?"

Evie shrugs. "Does it matter? The humans will want to gain Prince Albert's favor for the mere fact that he's human and a prince. They can't do that if they shun his wife. Besides, you will prove just how real your pairing is."

I quirk a brow. "There's more to this plan of yours?"

Her expression brightens. "In the two weeks between Prince Albert's arrival and your wedding date, you'll present your union to high society. A tour of sorts. You and Albert will attend the most respected social functions across the isle. Flaunt your latest fashions, all the ones you couldn't display at the showcase when the scandal erupted. You'll be sure to bring Bartleby's crawling back, begging you to attend the next showcase. But even if Bartleby's fails to see reason, you'll be presenting your work anyway. You'll become the most popular emerging designer in human fashion with or without that stuffy department store."

"Because I married a prince?" I say dryly.

Evie gives my shoulder a playful shrug. "No, because of *you*. Your prince will erase the scandal from everyone's minds, but the tour will demonstrate your artistry. That's all *you*, Ami."

Tears prick my eyes. I always knew Evie supported my career, as evidenced by her refusal to throw out the horrendous first creations I made for her. But this plan... it's smart. Not that I ever doubted Evie's brilliance. She's always been the intellectual one.

Her tone shifts to a more somber quality. "I'm not going to lie and say this tour idea doesn't benefit me too in some way. The Alpha Council wants us to pair Albert with someone we trust. Someone who can report on any suspicious activities before the marriage is finalized. If there's any sign that the offer of peace came with ulterior motives, the agreement is off."

"I am to spy on my own fiancé?"

Breeda kicks her legs against the backrest. "That sounds exciting!"

"To be blunt, yes," Evie says.

I ponder her scheme, seeking weaknesses. "If...if the peace offer seems genuine and I proceed with the marriage, must I...you know..."

She gives me a sympathetic frown. "He only has to be your husband in name. You know there are no rules regarding marital consummation in Faerwyvae anymore. No requirement that you must share a bedroom. You can keep your cottage and we can set him up in a manor of his own. So long as you present yourselves as a couple to the public eye, the marriage will suffice, both in the name of peace and to improve your reputation."

I swallow hard, my throat suddenly dry. "And what if he wants...more from our marriage? What if he doesn't take no for an answer?"

I shudder as hazy memories fill my mind. Of Cobalt compelling me to think I still loved him. I didn't get the chance to say no then, but I won't put myself in the position to be taken advantage of by a man ever again.

Evie's expression turns cold. "If he so much as touches you without permission, we'll kill him. Same goes for any suspicious actions he takes. King Grigory wants this alliance more than we do. I won't hesitate to kill his son." I know she means every word. Like me, Evie is no stranger to death and violence.

I sink back into the couch cushions. Can I do this? Can I marry a stranger to save my career? Evie was right when she said I'm famous amongst the fae. I could be satisfied with that.

But I didn't earn that fame on my own. Evie's notoriety is what gained me any kind of renown with the fae. I'm a bit irked that this new plan is all thanks to her too, not to mention how it hinges upon me having a royal husband.

My fashions, though, are all mine. Wearing them amongst high society, showing the humans that my artistry deserves a place in their closets...that will be *me*. Surely I can sign my name next to a prince's and tolerate his company in public. Right?

I release a slow exhale. "All right," I say before I can change my mind. "I'll do it."

"Goody!" Breeda says, clapping her hands. "I hope he's handsome."

Oh, for the love of the All of All, I've hardly given thought to the man himself. I haven't even seen the prince's portrait. When the Brettonish royals show up in Faerwyvae's scandal sheets, it's always through second-hand accounts. Roughly sketched reenactments. From what I've heard about Prince Albert, he's tall, handsome, and has golden hair. That, and he's a total drunkard.

I rub my brow. What am I getting myself into?

"Are you sure about this?" Evie asks, reading the distress on my face. "I know what I'm asking of you. You'd be giving up your chance to marry someone you actually love."

I bark a laugh. "That's not what I'm worried about."

My sister searches my face. When she speaks, her voice comes out quiet. "You deserve love, Ami. You know that, right?"

"I don't want love. Not everyone is as lucky as you and Aspen. Or Foxglove and Fehr. Or the dozens of other happy couples that seem to pop up all around me." I play it off with a chuckle, despite how my chest tightens. Ever since my grand disillusionment with romance, I've wondered if there is such a thing as real and healthy love. Could it really be as perfect as it looks on the outside? Are all these smitten couples hiding secrets, their relationships fraying at the seams like the Vances? Do their lovers coerce and control them? Hurt them over and over again? Because that's what love has looked like for me. As many times as Evie has tried to tell me that what I had with Cobalt wasn't love, it doesn't change that *he* thought it was. Even as Cobalt died in my arms, he professed to love me. After everything he did to me, after the abuse and lies, he somehow believed what he felt for me was love.

It's why I despise that word so greatly.

"If you're sure..." Evie says.

"I am," I say, tone resolute.

My sister looks almost sad, as if part of her hoped I'd fight her. That I'd insist on saving myself for a love match, not the cold façade this political union will be.

"Very well," she says. "I'll send word about our change of bride today. I can include the proposed tour in our agreement terms too. Or, if you would like to arrange it yourself, you can."

I ponder that for a moment. As much as I'd prefer to have no contact with my betrothed until necessary, if this involves my career, I want to take charge. "I'll do it. I'll write to him and request that he meets me for an engagement tour."

Breeda floats into the air with an elegant spin. "This is all so dreamy!"

"That's not what I'd call it," I mutter, but the sound is drowned out by a knock at the door. A second later, it opens to reveal a tall fae male with blue-black hair and a pair of antlers sprouting from his head.

King Aspen's eyes land on my sister. "Ah, there you are. A...um...a new table arrived." His lips curl into a crooked grin as he says the last part.

I bite the inside of my cheek to stifle my laugh. I know what *a new table* means. It's Evie and Aspen's secret code to proposition each other for romantic relations. Which happens...a lot around here. I don't think either of them know I've caught on by now, but I've certainly learned to make myself scarce when the word *table* is uttered.

"A new table," Evie says as she rises from the couch and meets her husband in the doorway. "We should go inspect it." Wrapping her arms around Aspen's neck, she stands on her tiptoes and greets him with a lingering kiss. Breeda flutters about them, staring at their locked lips with blatant fascination. I, on the other hand, avert my gaze, ignoring how my lungs feel suddenly too small. I'm not sure why my chest squeezes like this when I see couples together. It's not like I want what they have.

"You two should go inspect that table," I say as I rise to my feet. "Meanwhile, I'll write the letter to my betrothed."

Aspen's voice reaches my ears. "You agreed to the marriage?"

Now that they're no longer kissing, I can bear to look at them. I give him a pleasant smile. "Don't look so surprised. I am the agreeable sister, after all."

"That's for certain. This one, on the other hand..." He turns his gaze back to Evie, and his expression melts into something hopelessly sappy. Very few get to witness this side of the Stag King. To most, he's distant and stoic. But with my sister...

All right, I admit. Their dynamic is quite adorable.

"Is there a pen and paper in here?" I ask before their cuteness has a chance to turn smothering again.

Evie tilts her chin toward a cluttered corner. "There's a bureau over there. Are you sure you're all right with this whole...marriage thing?"

I give her a wry look and point out the door. "Go. Inspect. The table."

That's all the permission they need. As they close the door behind them, I march toward the corner Evie indicated, bypassing a small rocking chair filled to the brim with porcelain dolls, an ironing board displaying pocket watches, and a broken grandfather clock. Once I reach the bureau, I take a seat at the piano bench that stands before it and gather up a pen and sheet of paper. As I settle in to write, the paper takes on a red glow. Glancing up, I find Breeda is still here.

She lounges on the top of the bureau, idly twirling a strand of hair-like flame around her finger. "Oh, don't mind me. I want to witness the beginning of a love story up close."

I snort a laugh. "It doesn't look like this."

I bring the nib to the paper, noting how the sharp tip sinks into the sheet with a little too much force, as if I'm not writing to the prince but stabbing his heart. I grind my jaw as I scrawl the first line.

Dear Prince Albert...

4

For just over a week, my life seemed to go back to normal. No more incriminating photographs or headlines labeling me a hussy. Instead, my name showed up beside Prince Albert's in articles discussing the upcoming formal demonstration of peace between Faerwyvae and Bretton. Sure, some of these articles brought up my recent scandal, but it was overshadowed by all the other exciting tidbits—like speculations on what I'll wear on my wedding day, whether the event will be large or small, whether Prince Albert will prove to be as handsome as secondhand accounts suggest.

But as I stare down at the latest headline scrawled across the front page of today's *Hawthorn Hearsay*, I feel every inch of normalcy drain from my life at once. The title reads, *Desperate Debaucher Drowns Premarital Sorrows*. Beneath it is a black-and-white photograph of my betrothed sitting crookedly on a barstool, downing a pitcher of ale. Rivulets run down his chin and onto his waistcoat, giving the impression he's already well into his cups. Or...pitchers.

Ten other scandal sheets litter my drafting table, illuminated by the rising sun pouring into the windows of the downtown Hawthorn design studio I share with Foxglove. My friend isn't here yet, nor is anyone else from our design and manufacture teams. Thank the All of All for that, for I can't bear to see the look on anyone's faces when they see the other assorted headlines gracing the pages.

Prince Albert's Three-day Bender.

Bretton's Most Eligible Prince Becomes Faerwyvae's Most Miserable Barfly.

The Salty Satyr Pub Gains Wealthiest Patron.

Two Scandals and a Wedding.

They all have one thing in common: a theory that Albert is drinking so heavily because he dreads marrying me. Most bring up my scandal too, hypothesizing that the prince found out he was duped by being promised to spoiled goods.

Clenching my teeth, I gather up the papers. One slips out from the bottom of the stack. I stoop to pick it up and discover it's a letter I received yesterday. One that filled me with fiery rage upon reading it. After a week of anxiously awaiting Albert's reply to the engagement tour I proposed, he finally deigned to write back. Considering how quickly my sister received confirmation that King Grigory accepted a change of bride for the marriage alliance, Albert could have sent his own reply far sooner.

I crumple the papers in my fists until it forms a ball. Then I crush it between my palms, imagining it's Albert's puny head. While it's somewhat satisfying, it does little to lessen my anger. Every word of his insulting letter echoes through my head.

Dearest Miss Fairfield,

What a delight your little tour sounds. As lovely an offer as it is, I must regretfully decline, as I'd prefer to wait until our wedding day to cast my eyes upon your beautiful face. Until then, I'll dream of you, darling. I eagerly await meeting you at the end of the aisle.

Forever yours,
Albert

Rage pours through me, boiling my blood. When I first read the letter, I knew his soft words were nothing but empty flattery. I even suspected he harbored some hesitation about marrying me. But I didn't expect to find his idiotic face staring back at me from today's scandal sheets, silently boasting that his refusal wasn't delivered out of trepidation but a desire to drink himself stupid. It's...unacceptable. Disrespectful. Worst of all, it's embarrassing. Our pairing was supposed to save me from scandal, not plunge me deeper into it.

Another wave of anger courses through me, this time tingling from my chest and down my arms, filling my palms with heat. I release my rage in a roar, squeezing my ball of papers once more. But that's not all I release. The heat in my palms rises from a simmer to a blazing inferno. A flash of light fills my hands, surrounding the paper in bright red flames.

Surprise replaces my fury as the paper burns in my hands. It's been ages since I accidentally used my magic. My grandfather was a fire fae, which makes fire my primary elemental affinity. But flame isn't the only expression of the element. Fire also represents life force energy, passion, and creativity. While I'm fully capable of producing literal flame, I suppress the ability. I can still recall the terror in Evie's eyes when I first produced a flame in my palm. It was during the war, back when she'd yet to determine if I was still being controlled by Prince Cobalt. The way her face paled as she stared at what I'd created sent a shard of glass through my heart. One I still bear. Because I knew then she was afraid of me.

My relationship with my sister has improved since then, and I know she no longer fears me. Still, I prefer to channel my fire element through creativity, not flame.

I cast my eyes about my studio in a panic, desperate to keep my smoldering handful from spreading to the bolts of fabric, spools of thread, and the other flammable items surrounding me. Finally, I rush to the sink and drop the fiery mess into the porcelain basin. As I watch the scandal sheets burn, my rage and panic begin to fade, cooling like the ash now settling in the sink.

"I can handle this," I whisper to myself. If Albert is avoiding me because of the scandal with Mr. Vance, then this is my mess to fix. And if he's simply being indolent, then I'll save my rage for him.

I DID NOT DRESS FOR THE SUMMER COURT. THE realization hits me as soon as I leave the train station and step onto the streets of Port Dellaray, a city on the southern Summer Court coast. Despite being evening now, the humid heat surrounds me like a smothering shroud, making my silk hose cling uncomfortably to my legs. While I wore my chartreuse coat like I almost always do, I'm dressed in work attire beneath it. Thank the All of All I dressed in a simple wool skirt and linen blouse today instead of one of my more heavily layered day dresses.

After removing my coat and slinging it over my arm, I fan myself with one hand and head toward the heart of the city. There the streets grow crowded with patrons flooding in and out of restaurants, hotels, and public houses. Being one of two trade ports located in southern Faerwyvae, Port Dellaray is a busy town, bustling with dock workers, sailors, and merchants, both human and fae alike. However, since the ports fall under seelie jurisdiction, most of the fae here are in their seelie forms.

I stalk past storefronts and taverns with single-minded focus, seeking the name of the pub mentioned in the articles about Albert's drunken displays: The Salty Satyr. I find the pub on the street nearest the docks, which makes it one of the busiest but also least fashionable parts of town. The building itself is somewhat crude, with peeling paint and windows made of fogged glass that appears to be in good need of cleaning. What an odd choice for a prince. According to what Evie has told me, Albert was provided a suite at the finest hotel in Port Dellaray, which is several blocks from here. Additionally, my proposed tour included nightly stays at even finer establishments. If his only concern is drinking himself into a stupor, a luxury bar should be preferable to a second-rate public house.

Curling my fingers into fists, I pull open the door and march inside. The smell of smoke and ale fill my lungs at once, mingling with the stench of unwashed bodies after a hard day at work. The lighting is dim, and every table is full. I mostly find men dressed down to their shirtsleeves —dock workers—some with rounded human ears, others with pointed tips. A few show more obvious signs of fae heritage, including one man with seal flippers instead of hands and feet, and another with curling horns on each side of his head. I step farther into the crowded pub, noting not all patrons are of the working class. The closer I get to the bar, the more I note women in fine summer dresses and men with well-groomed mustaches in silk waistcoats.

No one seems to notice me as I brush past them, for their attention is fixed on something toward the back of the pub. Finally, I see what—or who—has them so magnetically entranced. At the very center of the bar sits a male with tousled golden hair, blue eyes, and a crooked smile set between two deep dimples. He's dressed in a fine gray suit, but his collar has been unbuttoned and his cravat hangs loose around his neck. With one arm slung across the bar top and his upper body careening to the side, he regales his captive audience with some slurred tale of a hunting party where he drunkenly fell asleep atop his horse and awoke in a den of angry boars. His admirers laugh and roar at his story, but I can't manage so much as a false smile.

My rage from this morning returns at full force, and it takes all my restraint not to let my palms catch fire like they did before. Channeling my inner flame into forti-tude, I storm straight up to my idiotic betrothed and pin him with a glare.

His words cut off abruptly as his eyes lock on mine.

He goes still, his expression drained of the smug joviality that painted it a moment before. For several beats, all he can do is blink at me. He must recognize me. While I've never seen an accurate portrait of him—save for what I discovered in the papers this morning—now that he's in Faerwyvae, it wouldn't be a challenge for *him* to find a picture of *me*. Whatever the case, he's so dumbstruck that he doesn't seem to notice himself listing to the side. Not until he nearly falls off his seat. As soon as he rights himself, his smirk is back, as are his dimples. He tilts his chin at me and sweeps his gaze over my form.

"What can I do you for?" he says, tone deep and slurred, each word tumbling into the next. Then, with an unsteady shake of his golden head, he corrects his state-ment, slower this time. "What I meant to say is, what can I do for you, you stunning creature? Or—if you're amenable—I meant what I said before too. I'd be happy to do you for nothing at all."

I ignore the last part and the way he waggles his brows. "What you can do is get off that stool and speak with me in there." I point to a closed door beneath a sign that says *Private Room—Reservations Only.*

His eyelids grow heavy as his grin widens. "No fore-play? Now, you're a lady who knows what she wants. At least tell me your name."

My cheeks burn with the heat of my growing anger. Does that mean he doesn't recognize me after all? Whether he does or doesn't, this exchange goes beyond humiliating. How many other women has he so brazenly propositioned in front of amused spectators when he's supposed to be engaged to me? Every muscle in my body goes tense at how many witnesses stand before us now.

I take a step closer and lower my voice. "I'm your fiancée, you empty-headed ogre."

"Ogre," he says with a chuckle. "That's a first. Most people call me Your Highness."

"You're no prince of my country, which means I'll call you what I like."

Whispers surround us, but I force myself to ignore them. Instead, I wave at the barkeep, who stands frozen with his dishrag buried in the glass he's pretending to clean. With a startled jolt at my attention, he approaches the bar.

I speak before he can. "I need that room. Now."

His mouth falls open as his gaze darts between me and the private room. "It's...it's reservations only—"

"This is my reservation," I say, pushing a large coin across the table. On one side, it bears the letters *EF*, my sister's initials. On the other is her profile. Royal coins are symbols that inform their recipients that the owner of said coin is not to be argued with and that any expenses involved are to be charged to the court indicated by the coin itself. Evie may not have power in the Summer Court, but all royals are to be respected across the isle. And while it crushes my pride to use my sister to get my way, now is not the time for ego. Not when I'm seconds away from burning the prince to a crisp.

The barkeep's eyes go wide. He returns the coin to me with a fervent nod. "The room is yours, miss."

I turn my gaze to my fiancé and find him slowly sliding off his stool, a look of mild terror in his eyes. Or is it awe? Then he shutters his expression and dons that lazy smirk, extending a hand toward the private room. "After you, gorgeous."

I sweep past him only to halt after a few steps. He pulls up short, nearly colliding with me. I round on him and stand tall, chin lifted, while he stumbles to regain steady footing. "Call me that again," I say through my teeth, "and I'll burn out your tongue."

To his credit, he doesn't so much as blanch. Instead, his eyes fall to my lips. "Mmm. I like a woman with a little fire."

Heat floods my palms once more, but this time it rises to my cheeks too. Before he can see my angry blush, I whirl around and enter the private room.

5

Prince Albert and I sit across from each other at a circular table, him in a cushioned booth, me in a leather high-backed chair. The room is modest in size, large enough to host business meetings but quaint enough to ensure only one party at a time may utilize it. The lighting here is dimmer than it was in the main part of the pub, with dark, windowless walls surrounding us and single brass chandelier hanging over the table.

Albert shifts anxiously in his seat, his expression fluctuating between his carefree smirk and something more somber. We haven't spoken since settling into the room. He seems to be giving me the chance to talk first, and I'm still trying to cool my rage.

"So, you're my fae bride," Albert finally says, giving up on silence. When I don't reply, he adds, "You don't look fae. No pointed ears. No fangs. No claws."

If I weren't so angry, I'd tell him I can relate to such preconceived notions. There was a time when I too thought all fae were monstrous beasts. "And you don't look like a prince. No manners. No poise. No gentility."

He huffs a laugh. "You aren't what I was expecting at all."

"Imagine my disappointment at discovering the same about you."

A small wooden panel set above a wide shelf opens in one of the walls, revealing the face of the barkeep. "Drinks?" he asks, tone hesitant.

"A bottle of wine," I say, keeping my gaze on Albert. "Agave Ignitus, please."

The prince leans back in his booth, crossing an ankle over his knee and draping one arm along the backrest. "I like wine."

I narrow my eyes. "One glass. That's all. Thank you."

The barkeep slides the panel shut, and Albert juts out his lower lip in a mock pout. "None for me? I promise to behave."

"Your promise means nothing."

"No? Are we not set to make vows very soon, fiancée of mine?"

It takes no small amount of control to keep my voice level. "I'm having second thoughts about whether I want to make those vows at all anymore."

His smile slips, and his entire body goes taut.

Good. That means threats to our impending marriage have an effect on him. I continue to stare down my betrothed as we wait for the barkeep to return. Until I've swallowed at least a glass of wine, I don't trust myself to keep my cool.

While I'm fighting to maintain my composure, the prince is actively losing his. With every second that ticks by, Albert appears to grow more and more anxious. His leg begins to bounce while he taps his fingers against the backrest of the booth. He keeps his body in a casual slouch, but there's a tenseness to his carefree posture. His eyes wander about the room, but like a magnet, they snap back to mine again and again. Each time, I meet them with a glare.

When he's had enough of my staring, he lifts his arm and pulls back the sleeve of his gray jacket. A string of red berries encircles his wrist. "I'm wearing rowan, so if you're trying to use your fae magic to glamour me with compulsion, it won't work."

I blink a few times, caught off guard by his accusation. "That's...that's not what I was doing. I would never compel anyone. Not only is it illegal, but it's...it's cruel." I hate the way my voice trembles when I say the last part, but my words are true. As someone who's been the victim of compulsion, I know just how vile it is. I clear my throat to steady my voice. "Humans are protected from compulsion here. Saint John's Wort is added to communal drinking water, and almost everyone wears some form of rowan berry. Just...just don't give anyone your true name."

He tilts his head to the side. "Is it true everyone has a secret name here, and only discovering this name gives a fae power over a human?"

"No, that's a myth. It's far simpler than that. If you outright state to a fae that you *give them your true name*, using those exact words, that ignites the magic. That is the only way a fae can forcibly compel you. It overrides all other safeguards that may be in place. So never say those words."

What I don't tell him is that I have personal experience with giving away the power of my name. It's exactly how I was compelled by Prince Cobalt in the first place.

Albert flutters his too-long lashes at me. "Aww. Concerned about my well-being, dearest?"

I bristle at his jesting tone, realizing I momentarily let my guard down with him. Thankfully, I'm saved from coming up with a barbed retort by the return of the barkeep. He opens the panel and sets my glass and bottle on the shelf beneath it, then slides the little door shut.

I collect my libation, pouring as I return to my seat, then down a glass before I've fully settled at the table. The Agave Ignitus wine warms my belly at once, satisfying my fire with its pleasantly scalding liquor. I pour another.

When I glance back at the prince, he's grinning like an idiot. "You seem to have a healthy thirst for spirits. A woman after my own heart."

"Don't talk to me about hearts," I say, gratified that I'm able to keep my tone calm. "I know our union isn't a love match, and I neither want nor expect it to be."

He frowns for the briefest instant before donning that flippant grin of his. "I take it you're upset with me for refusing to attend the engagement tour you planned for us."

I shake my head and take a drink from my wineglass. "Your refusal is something I could almost understand. It's your actions I can't abide by. Do you even want this marriage? To forge peace between Bretton and Faerwyvae?"

"Yes," he says, and I'm surprised by the conviction in his tone. "It is my utmost priority."

I bark a laugh. "Priority? Based on what I've seen in the scandal sheets, your priority has been making a fool of our upcoming nuptials by drinking yourself into a stupor. Have you no sense of pride? No concern over your reputation or mine?"

He taps his fingers on the backrest, leg bouncing again. The way his lips are pursed tight makes me think he's fighting against saying something. But as he leans forward and lunges for the bottle of wine, I realize he wasn't fighting with words but his craving for drink. He spirits it across the table before I can even think of trying to wrest it back.

He presses the bottle to his lips, long enough for several deep pulls, then lets the bottleneck hang between his fingers. "This has nothing to do with you. I'm simply... enjoying myself."

I pull my head back. "Nothing to do with me? Are you mad? This has everything to do with me. Everyone knows you're my fiancé. You've gotten yourself plastered over the front page of every scandal sheet across the isle. Do you know who they bring up in each article? *Me*—the very reason you're drinking so much, according to reporters. I understand if that's true. Honestly, I do. I remember what it was like the first time I was forced into an arranged pairing. I recall my terror at the thought of marrying a fae—"

I bite off my words. I've ventured into personal territory he doesn't need to know about. I seek a shift in subject that still expresses what I need to convey. "I understand your reservations, your animosity. You've probably been told things about faekind that aren't true. And I realize that being forced to wed me, in particular, can't be ideal. You may have heard about...my past. A certain recent scandal. It's false, mind you, and...and..." I catch my breath, realizing I'm rambling. Where did my careful composure go?

I take another long drink from my wineglass, no longer holding his gaze. Instead, my eyes fall on the table between us. "I know I'm much older than you—"

"Old?" he says with a scoff. "You can be however old, darling. You don't look a day over stunning."

"Please stop calling me that," I say, my tone more tired than anything. "Darling, gorgeous. Just save the false flattery. That's not what I want from you."

Silence stretches between us. Then, "All right."

His soft tone has me meeting his eyes again.

"I'm not doing this," he nods at the bottle of wine still dangling from his fingers, "because of you. I'm not drinking because I have reservations about our union. Regardless of what it looks like, forging peace is my priority."

I frown, noting the sudden clarity in his speech, the straightening of his slumped posture. "Then what is it about?"

His eyes search mine for several long seconds, and I can't help noticing things about him I hadn't before. Like his sharp jaw dotted with stubble, his slightly overlarge nose. The lump at its bridge makes it look as if it's been broken. Contrasting such a rough feature are his crystal-blue eyes and his beautiful golden tresses that fall over his forehead in a devil-may-care style that looks too good to be anything but calculated.

He shifts in his seat, snapping me out of my inspection. I shake my head to clear it. Why was I bothering to assess his appearance? It's not like it matters what my future husband looks like, only that he improves my reputation and saves my career. Which he's so far managed to make worse.

"I'm sorry," he says. "I didn't realize my actions were affecting you in such a way. I promise you, it hadn't crossed my mind."

I narrow my eyes. He didn't answer my question.

He sets the wine bottle on the table like a peace offering. "Will you forgive me?"

Part of me is tempted to argue more, to make him fully understand what's at stake for me. But reminding him of his own stakes might be far more persuasive.

I stand and reach into my skirt pockets, extracting five leather pouches. One by one, I drop them on the table with a thump. "This is the currency for the five courts we'll be visiting on our engagement tour. It's more than enough to cover train fare between each court, as well as cab fare, food, and spending money. Your hotels have been booked and paid for. You will stay in them, and you will do your drinking and debauching in private, far from the public eye. To society, we will present ourselves as the happy couple we need to be. Here is your itinerary."

I take the last item from my pocket—a copy of our tour schedule, which I already sent in my first letter to him—and push it across the table.

He opens his mouth to speak, but I cut him off.

"You *will* attend this tour. Sober. That is how you'll earn my forgiveness. More importantly, that is the only way I will go through with our marriage. The only way peace between Faerwyvae and Bretton will be brokered. Don't even think about requesting a change of bride.

After this little display you've pulled, I doubt any well-bred relative of fae royalty would have you now."

I don't know which of my words are a bluff, if any, but they seem to have their intended effect.

With a resigned sigh, he gathers up the itinerary. His eyes go wide, and he lifts his gaze to mine. "The first event is tomorrow night."

I gather my coat off the back of my chair and drape it over my arm. "Catch the first train to the Jasper City Station tomorrow. Pick me up in a coach-and-four at eight p.m. at the Foxhollow Hotel. Don't be late."

His smirk returns, as do his infuriating dimples. "Leaving so soon? We haven't finished our bottle of wine yet." Once again, his words are jumbled together. How does he switch so seamlessly between being sloshed and serious?

I whirl away from him and stride toward the door. "I have a train to catch."

He springs to my side. "Shouldn't we...you know, exit as a happy couple?"

I pause, fingers on the door handle. He's right. That's exactly what we should do. But I don't think I can feign anything close to premarital bliss right now.

When I don't answer, he leans in closer. "Not even a goodnight kiss before our audience?"

Clenching my jaw, I open the door. "Goodnight, Your Highness."

Before I can step over the threshold, his fingers come around mine. I'm too startled to pull away, even more so when he whirls me around to face him. His eyelids are heavy, mouth quirked in a roguish smile as he bends over my hand. Then, with featherlight pressure, he alights a kiss on the back of my hand. My breath hitches at the feeling of his lips through my lace gloves.

A bright light blares into the side of my face. With a startle, I whirl toward the crowd that watches us. Another flash of light sparks before me, and when it dims, I notice a boxlike contraption held in a fae male's hand. His other holds a stick with a large bulb at the end. I didn't see the photographer when I first arrived, so he must have come while Albert and I were speaking. Behind him, two figures scrawl furiously in their notebooks. Reporters. Damn.

Something squeezes my fingers. A glance back at Albert reminds me he's still holding my hand. He's no longer bent over it, but standing tall, a glowing smile stretching from ear to ear. "Goodnight, Amelie Fairfield," he says, not bothering to lower his voice.

It's the first time he's said my name, and the sound of it rumbling in his deep tone has my pulse quickening.

"Until tomorrow," he says, then lets my fingertips slip from his own.

Belatedly, I tug my hand in front of me, hiding it in the folds of my coat. Then, with a forced smile for our wide-eyed spectators, and not a single backwards glance for Prince Albert, I leave the pub and make a beeline for the train station. My aggravation grows with every step I take, for no matter how I try to brush off my gloves, my hand won't cease tingling with the warmth of Albert's lips.

6

The next evening at a quarter to eight, I stand outside the Foxhollow Hotel in the Earthen Court, awaiting Prince Albert's arrival. I half expect him not to show. There's even a part of me that hopes he doesn't. For if that's the case, I can refuse to proceed with our marriage, and this can all be over. But that's not the only thing that will come to an end. My career is still at stake. If we dissolve our arranged nuptials now, I'll be seen as the cause. Scandal surrounding my name will never die down.

At least today's papers have been mostly positive. While a few have reported upon last night's icy first encounter between me and Albert at the Salty Satyr, the majority are more focused on the farewell kiss he planted on my hand. Since the latter story has photographic evidence to support it, it's the most popular.

When I first saw my name in today's headlines, I braced myself for the worst, especially when I caught my first glimpse of the photograph. But the longer I studied it, the more shocked I was by the deceptively romantic image it depicted. With how I'm angled slightly away from the photographer, I don't look as shocked or terrified as I was in the moment. Instead, the focus is on Albert, on his lips hovering an inch from my hand, his gaze locked on mine as he watches me from under his lashes. To anyone who didn't know better, he appears enchanted with me. And from the way I stand frozen, my lips slightly parted, I look charmed.

This is the first time a photograph has served me well with its ability to steal a moment devoid of context and twist it into a lie. Perhaps I'll clear my name after all.

That is, if Albert ever shows.

I extract a pocket watch from inside my blue silk purse. It's still ten minutes to eight, so I can't consider Albert late yet. I return the pocket watch to my purse, straighten my gloves, brush out my skirt, and do anything that distracts me from the fact that I'm about to have dinner with my future husband. I haven't been on a date with a man since before everything that happened with Prince Cobalt. Not that tonight's date is a real one. It's an act. Pretend.

With a man I will soon be married to.

I shove that thought from my mind and focus on what's most important—that tonight is my first chance to show off one of my designs. It's an evening gown with sapphire blue velvet on the bodice, bustle, and overskirt. My underskirt is a pale blue floral-patterned silk draped in tiered layers and pinned with white rosettes. I've paired the dress with all the trappings meant to evoke human propriety, both seen and unseen—corset, silk hose, dinner gloves—as well as an updo that already has my scalp aching.

I'm not normally a fan of wearing my hair up, nor do I tend to favor so many layers of clothing. Instead, I prefer to wear my hair down and don attire in the light, flowing fae style, or even the more simplistic human skirts and blouses. But if my plan is to work, I must wear my designs myself and show them off in all their stunning glory.

Just when I'm about to check the time again, a sleek black coach-and-four approaches where I stand outside the hotel. Night has fully fallen, so I can't make out who sits behind the glass windows, but as it stops before me, I'm certain it's Albert. Relief and dread fill me at once.

A footman descends from the rear of the coach to open the door for me. With a deep breath that does nothing to lessen the quickening of my pulse, I enter the coach. The prince sits on the rear seat, so I take the bench across from him, arranging the heavy folds of my skirt before I force myself to look at him. If he appears even slightly inebriated—

I'm momentarily stunned as I take in the man across from me. I almost don't recognize the prince, with his black frock coat over a white waistcoat, shirt, and tie, all done up properly without a single button out of place. In one gloved hand, he holds a black gentleman's cane, while his golden hair is partially obscured by a top hat. The only thing that gives him away as the same insuffer-able man I spoke to last night is his crooked grin embedded between those mocking dimples.

"You look rather lovely, Miss Fairfield," Albert says, looking me over.

I open my mouth, but instead of accepting the

compliment, I avert my gaze out the window. The coach has begun to move, giving me a receding view of my hotel, followed by a glimpse of rolling hills in the distance. They're nothing but black silhouettes against the night sky now, but during the day, the city of Jasper is gorgeous. Nestled in a valley between the lush mountains the Earthen Court is famous for, Jasper has become one of the most popular human cities on the isle. It isn't a large city, though, so it won't be long until we reach our destination. Which means I must say what I've been planning to all day.

"Prince Albert," I say, forcing my attention back to him, "we need to establish ground rules."

He leans back in his seat, losing some of his sophisticated composure, and props an ankle over his knee. "I thought we did so last night?"

"I mean for the entirety of our marriage. There are certain things I want to make clear before we take this arrangement of ours one step further."

"Very well. What are these ground rules?"

I hold his gaze, trying my best not to be put off by his ceaseless grin, and deliver my first rule. "For starters, we will only be married in name. We will not consummate our marriage. We will own property together, but we will spend much of our time apart."

"Did I truly make such a poor impression on you?" he says with a chuckle.

"Never lie to me," I say, ignoring his question. "You may keep your private doings to yourself. No need to keep me apprised of every last thing you do, but if I ask, be honest. That's my one steadfast rule. No lies. The rest of what I said last night applies to our marriage. Keep any unsavory behavior away from the public eye, but do maintain an image of marital bliss before society. Do nothing that compromises my reputation. Do you agree?"

His smile slips into a frown, his brow knitting into a furrow. "Is there no part of you that wants a true marriage?"

"No," I say, wrenching my gaze back to the window. Mountainous silhouettes have been replaced by the tightly clustered buildings and storefronts of downtown Jasper. "Our marriage is a political union. It would be foolish to expect more than that. For *either* of us to expect more."

"Have you never heard of an arranged marriage that resulted in love?"

I want to deny it...but I can't. My sister's marriage is a true love match, and that love was born from a political arrangement. Then again, I was the one who was originally paired with her husband. My treachery brought them together. In a way, I can't regret that. Evie has reminded me of that fact on several occasions. Probably just to lessen my guilt.

In lieu of a true answer, I say, "My career is the most important thing to me."

"Ah. You're a fashion designer, correct?"

"Yes, and I can't let you do anything that compromises that. Right now, my priority is growing my career in the human market. I can't do that if I'm depicted as a woman married to a drunken debaucher. You, being a human prince, should understand the importance of image, virtue, and reputation when it comes to gaining other humans' respect."

"I am sorry, Amelie." His somber tone paired with the

sound of my name on his lips has my eyes returning to him. "Truly, I am. I never meant to cause you or your career harm."

My heart thuds under the weight of his gaze. There's genuine apology in his eyes. His voice. His bearing. It's... it's too real.

"Everything we do is fake," I say in a rush. "Understand that. Whatever we do in public...none of that shall happen between us behind closed doors."

He assesses me through slitted lids, as if he's trying to read between my words. I keep my expression neutral, posture steady, so he'll realize there's nothing to decipher. Nothing hidden behind my efforts to keep him at arm's length.

Nothing.

Not even the gnawing sensation that claws my stomach or the hollow ache buried deep in my heart.

Finally, his demeanor returns to its carefree façade. "You don't have to worry about me falling in love with you," he says with a wink.

I choose my next words carefully. "I'm talking about more than that. I've heard about your...your reputation with women. And I...well, when it comes to the types of things married couples do, you and I...we won't be doing those things."

"I see," he says, a hint of amusement playing around his lips. "Do you not do *those things* at all?"

A blush of heat floods my cheeks. "I don't have to answer that."

He gives me a pointed look. "You requested that I never lie to you when asked a question. I think I should be allowed the same respect."

"But *those things* are private."

"As are my—how did you put it? Drunken debauching? Yes, such activities of mine are private too, and yet you've made them the topic of our conversation more than once now."

"And you've made them the topic of everyone's conversation by making a public spectacle of yourself. That isn't what I call private, Your Highness." I say his title with clear mocking.

"Well played, Miss Fairfield. Still, if we are to be married and I am to participate in this grand charade of ours, I do insist on the same level of candor you expect from me. So tell me. Do you or do you not do *those things*?" When I don't answer, he elucidates. "Lovemaking. Kissing. Canoodling—"

"Yes," I bite out. "I...I participate in such activities when the need drives me. Sometimes...alone. Other times with a partner. A temporary one." Oh, for the love of the All of All, why am I even telling him this? There was once a time when talk of sex and sensuality made me feel bold. I spoke about my evening exploits and flirtations the way most people talk about the weather. But those days are long gone. I've learned what dark paths lie at the end of lust and romance, and I never want to walk them again. Or talk about them at all.

He narrows his eyes. "I see. The matter at hand is you don't want to do those things with *me*. Partially because you dislike me, but more so because we are to be married. There's nothing temporary about that, is there? So you'd like to ensure we never cross the line into physical intimacy because you prefer the occasional dalliance over a deep relationship."

I purse my lips. Since when does the playboy prince have the mind of a private investigator?

He wags a gloved finger at me. "I'm right, aren't I?"

I hide my growing discomfort behind a seething grin. "Don't presume to know me, Highness."

"Oh, I wouldn't dare to presume a thing about you, darling."

I clamp my jaw tight. "I thought I told you—"

"To dispose of the false flattery? I know. But I'm afraid it can't be avoided if we want to put on a proper show." He gestures toward the window, and I realize the coach has stopped.

All prior thoughts flee from my mind as I stare out at the small crowd gathered outside a quaint stone structure bearing a sign that reads *The Golden Stone*. It's the restaurant where Albert and I will be spending our first evening as a couple in the public eye. My pulse kicks up at the sight of so many people waiting to be let inside. Thankfully, Albert and I have reservations, but it doesn't calm my nerves. I try to remind myself that the more people the better. I need to be seen—both in my ensemble and with my fiancé—for this tour to have the effect I intend. Despite telling myself this, I can't bear to move as the footman opens the coach door.

Thankfully, Albert is quicker to act. He steps out of the coach and turns to me with an open palm. A few people from the crowd turn curious glances our way. Lowering his voice, he leans forward. "Ready to dazzle, Miss Fairfield?"

I swallow hard and place my hand in his.

7

As soon as we're seated inside the restaurant, I realize my mistake. Not only is this my first public outing with Albert, but it's my first step into the public eye since the scandal erupted. Every day since my name first graced the headlines, I've kept my focus on work and spent most of my time either at my studio or my cottage. I've shopped, held meetings, seen clients, and interacted with my design team, but nothing more than what is already part of my weekly routine. I haven't so much as set foot at a society function.

The grand opening of the newest upscale restaurant in the most popular human city in the Earthen Court is certainly a society event. That was the whole point, of course, but I failed to account for how anxious I'd be. Or how many sets of eyes look our way. How many lips whisper behind their hands.

Are they whispering because there's a prince in their midst? Or because he's with me, an alleged husband-stealing harlot?

My only solace is that the restaurant is dim. The walls and ceiling are comprised of dark slate, evoking a cave-like atmosphere. Artful water fixtures are interspersed along the walls to give the illusion of trickling waterfalls. A few simple lightbulbs hang from climbing ivy, but most of the light comes from the glowing green sprites that flutter overhead. If I weren't so nervous, I'd be impressed by the decor and the way it utilizes natural elements—something that would normally appeal more to the fae—in a way that is considered safe and charming to human clientele.

"Relax." Albert's whispered voice steals my attention. He sits across from me in a wooden chair that matches my own. Both seats retain some organic shape provided by the trees they were carved from. The armrests are curved branches, the legs spindly roots. A roughly hewn stone table stands between us set with dishes, napkins, and flatware.

I blink at him. Now that he's without his top hat, he looks a little more like his roguish self with the way his golden locks fall lazily about his face. Unlike me, he doesn't seem at all perturbed by the whispers uttered from nearby tables. "I'm plenty relaxed," I mutter, keeping my voice low to avoid being overheard.

"You look as taut as a bowstring." He takes a hearty drink of his wine—the only thing we've been served so far—which earns him a scowl from me. If he turns into a befuddled buffoon, I will kill him.

"I'm simply..." I seek a lie that sounds believable. Not that I owe him an explanation. "Hungry."

He swirls his glass, sending the ruby-colored liquid

swishing, and arches a brow. "You look like you want to strangle me."

"This isn't about you," I say. Just then a woman at the nearest table lets out a giggle, followed by a hushed string of words to her dinner companion that end in something that sounds an awful lot like *married man*. She must be talking about me. About the scandal. Why did Evie think marrying a prince would make it all go away? What if... what if this is just making it worse? And...is that a reporter sitting at the corner table? A female figure sits alone, jotting things down in a notebook. When she lifts her gaze from her page, her eyes lock on me and Albert, her lips quirked into a sly grin. She resumes writing, her pace faster now.

"Hey." Again, Albert's voice snags my attention. "Are you all right?"

The sudden concern in his eyes has me bristling. "I'm fine."

He watches me, brow furrowed, for a few moments longer before donning his carefree grin. Setting his glass on the table, he leans toward me. "Your body language is all wrong."

"Body language? What does that—"

"If you want to convince everyone that we're madly in love, then you need to change your posture. Don't sit straight. Don't look away from me. Sit closer. Lean in. Angle your body toward me as if it's magnetically drawn to mine." He says it with an easy smile, his voice barely above a whisper. To anyone looking our way, he probably appears to be uttering sweet nothings, not discussing my rigid posture.

Heat rises to my cheeks. Not at what he's suggesting...

but because he's right. I used to know these things. I used to *do* these things. Naturally. Inherently. No one was off limits for flirtation, and I bandied about my sexuality as easily as breathing. But now...

I've lost that part of me. Buried it. For good reason too.

But if I want to wipe my scandal from everyone's minds, I need to give them something else to talk about. Something positive. Romantic. Like that meaningless kiss he planted on my hand.

Despite knowing what I must do, I can't bring myself to do it.

Before I realize what's happening, Albert rises from his chair and rounds the table toward me. "You must forgive me, my dear, for I did not properly push in your chair for you when we first sat down. Please allow me to remedy my shortcomings." This time, his words are loud enough to be heard by those around us.

I'm not sure what he's on about, but I stand and allow him to pull out my chair.

"Take a step closer to the table," he whispers.

I do, pulling my skirts along with me. When he slides my chair toward my legs, I sink back down. Now I'm several inches closer to the table. I expect Albert to return to his seat, but instead, I feel his gloved hand fall upon my shoulder, resting at the base of my cap sleeve. My breath hitches at the unexpected touch. I angle my face toward him and find him smiling down at me.

"That's better, isn't it, dearest? Now you won't feel as if you're a million miles away from me." When I don't reply, he gives my shoulder a soft squeeze and returns to his seat. Once he's settled back in, he leans forward again.

This time, he extends his hand across the table, palm up. "Lean in and place your hand in mine," he says under his breath.

My heart slams against my ribs at such an absurd request. But his little stunt with the chair has drawn even more attention to us. I can't look as if I reject his affections.

Donning what I hope looks like a sweet smile, I lean forward and drape my arm halfway across the table until our gloved hands meet.

"You still look like you want to strangle me," he says, tone soft despite the warning his words carry.

I match his pitch and speak through my forced grin. "If I didn't before, I certainly do now."

He laughs, loud enough to carry. "You're hilarious, Miss Fairfield." Then, back to a whisper, he says, "You're still stiff. Loosen your arm. Lean in a little more."

"You try leaning across a table in a corset and dinner gown."

He waggles his brows. "If that's what gets you going, I will, although you'll find I look better naked."

A huff of air escapes my mouth. It takes me several seconds to realize it was a laugh. Not only that, but my lips have curled into a genuine grin. But as I recall what he said to amuse me, I swallow my mirth. I have no reason to believe his words were said in anything but jest, yet I can't risk him thinking such subjects are appropriate between us. Not when he is to be my husband. Until I know for certain that he understands exactly what we are and what we're not, I can't have him saying such—

"Miss Fairfield." The voice comes not from Albert but

a man standing beside our table. It's a familiar tone, one that turns my blood to ice.

Slowly, I turn to face Howard Vance.

Rage replaces the ice in my blood as I look into the face of the man who brought scandal into my life. He's a middle-aged man with a stout figure, thinning hair, several chins, and beady eyes. "Mr. Vance," I say curtly. "I wasn't aware you and Maureen would be here tonight."

It's true. If I'd known, I wouldn't have come. I knew I'd eventually have to face the Vances, but I hoped it wouldn't be tonight—what was supposed to be the easiest stop on our engagement tour.

"I wasn't expecting you either, although I was hoping I'd see you again eventually." His eyes bore into me, paying not an ounce of respect to my royal companion. He angles himself closer to me and lowers his voice. "We never did get to finish those...measurements you were supposed to take. Shall I make an appointment this time?"

My rage grows hotter, even more so when a flurry of whispers breaks out from the tables around us. Fire laces my palms, begging to be unleashed. How dare he be so presumptuous!

I feel pressure on my fingers and realize Albert is still holding my hand. I meet his eyes and feel as if a lock has sprung open in my mind. All my buried instincts flood me at once, turning my stiff arms loose, my posture easy. Flinging my other hand across the table to meet my other, I gather Albert's palm between both of mine. Leaning forward, I arch my back slightly and lift my chest, letting the cut of my bodice do all the rest of the work to put my cleavage on display. In a few subtle shifts of my bearing, I now look the part of a woman who is positively infatuated with the man sitting across from her.

"Mr. Vance, have you met my fiancé, Prince Albert?" My voice is airy as I speak, my eyes trained on the prince all the while, as if I can't bear to look away from him for even a moment. "We're getting married in two weeks."

"That's right," Albert says, turning his gaze to Mr. Vance. "So you must forgive my future bride for not having any time for new clients."

I hazard a glance at Mr. Vance to find his face has gone beet red. "I'm hardly a new client. Miss Fairfield has been working for my wife for months."

I'm about to remind him that his wife dissolved our working relationship, but Albert speaks first.

"And you'll have to forgive me for not wanting to share my fiancée's attention with any other man tonight. Thank you for introducing yourself and for your warm wishes over our upcoming nuptials." Then, with a dismissive wave that makes him seem every inch the privileged prince he must have been hiding all along, he returns his full attention to me.

Mr. Vance and I are both robbed of words, but after a few tense beats of silence, our interloper storms off.

Whispers surround us once more. For the love of the All of All, rumors will fly about what just occurred. If not carried by our fellow diners, then certainly by the reporter. But will I be shown in a positive light? Or a negative one?

"Ignore them," Albert says. "We won that round."

The way he says *we,* like we're truly a team, sends my heart skittering. Is this what it feels like to be in a romantic partnership? Like it's two against the world? I remind myself this is all pretend. He's only doing what I asked him to do.

Regardless, some of the ire I've held against him softens. Perhaps there's more than one side to the prince than the liquor-addled lush the scandal sheets presented. He hasn't ceased being a shameless flirt, but if he can manage to only flirt with me and not every female in existence...well, this might just work.

"You called that man Mr. Vance," Albert says, rousing me from my thoughts. "Is he Howard Vance of Vance Industries?"

"Yes," I say. I'm surprised he knows the name, considering he's a prince from another country. The Vances may be an elite family here, but I doubt they matter much to Brettonish royalty. Then again, I suppose Vance Industries has made a name for itself through whatever it is they manufacture, and this marriage alliance is all about improving trade.

Albert takes up his wine glass with his free hand and downs a long drink. "I didn't take you as someone who associates with crime bosses."

I pull my head back. "Crime bosses? What do you mean?"

"Vance Industries got its start as a front for the opium trade, did it not? I suppose they're a legitimate business now, but that wasn't always the case."

I open my mouth but don't know what to say. Opium trade? While I know opium dens exist in Faerwyvae, there are plenty of substances made from special fae fruits on the isle that offer similar intoxicating effects for a fraction of the consequences. Not all, of course. There are an equal number of fae fruits that will kill a human with a single bite, but those plants are heavily protected and regulated. Still, the Vances are a well-respected family. They couldn't have gotten their start by having ties to organized crime, could they?

No, of course not. Besides, how would Albert know about it? He's only been here a handful of days, while this has been my home for decades.

"Are those the kinds of stories they tell in Bretton about the isle?" I ask. "I expected sordid tales of vicious beasts, changelings, and soul-sucking monsters."

"Oh, we get plenty of those stories too. In fact, I expected you to have wings, gills, and fangs." He sets down his wineglass and brings his hand in front of his lips, miming curved fangs with his fingers.

I snort a laugh. "Did no one tell you I'm only a quarter fae?"

"A quarter fae and one hundred percent beautiful? Nope. No one said a damn thing to warn me about you." He winks, and it makes my belly tighten.

My eyes fall to our hands still clasped together at the center of the table. All at once, I release his palm and straighten in my seat. My body feels hot and cold at the same time, my cheeks flushed, my palms tingling, my chest filled with ice.

He frowns and slowly pulls his hand back to his side of the table. "Did I say something wrong?" he whispers.

It takes no small effort to sort through my words. "I... I'm still not used to your flatteries, that's all." While it's true, I'm not sure that's the real problem. I think I'm more worried over the chance that genuine attraction could be behind his compliments. Or—at the very least—rakish lust. And I very well can't have that.

"You did well," he says, flashing his dimples with a smile that doesn't reach his eyes. "I think we have them convinced for now."

I sneak a glance around and find no scandalized faces looking back at us. A few peek our way, but most look mildly intrigued. Envious, at worst. Relief uncoils inside me, but it's short-lived. Our meal hasn't even been served yet.

"Best of all," he says, eyeing me from over the rim of his wineglass, "I finally got to hear you laugh."

8

The rest of our dinner passes with relative ease. We're served a fine meal, we make small talk, and I don't catch sight of the Vances again. I'm still too anxious to taste my dinner, but I get the impression it would be delicious, were I in a more relaxed state. By the time we leave and retrieve our belongings from the coatroom—my coat and his hat and cane—I'm filled with a bone-deep exhaustion.

"That went swimmingly, if you ask me," Albert says as we exit the front door and make our way toward the waiting coach-and-four. The footman descends from the back of the coach, but Albert waves him off and opens the door for me himself.

"It did," I say as I climb inside. "I'm a little surprised, to be honest."

He puts a hand to his chest and pretends to stumble back. "Ouch. Was your first impression of me really so terrible?"

I give him a pointed look. "Yes."

"Fair enough," he says with an exaggerated sigh. Then his expression turns more serious. Still outside the coach, he props his cane under his arm and leans slightly forward. "I hope I'm earning your forgiveness."

My heart constricts in a strange way. Part of me wants to thank him for making our first date so tolerable, but I keep my tone neutral. "Today was a good start."

"Then I'll prove myself again at our next tour stop." He tips his hat but makes no move to enter the coach. "Good evening—"

"You're not coming too?"

Averting his gaze from me, he takes his cane out from under his arm and plants its tip on the ground. Then, with a deep inhale, he makes a show of breathing in the evening air. "No, I think I'll walk back to my hotel. It's a lovely night for a starlit stroll."

I narrow my eyes, a spike of suspicion replacing my previously placid mood. Scooting to the edge of my seat until I'm leaning halfway out the door, I cast a glance around the sidewalk. Once I'm certain no restaurant patrons loiter about close by, I lower my voice and speak in a hiss. "You're sneaking off to a pub, aren't you? After that little speech about forgiveness."

He pulls his head back. "Of course not. I truly am just taking a walk."

I shake my head with a mirthless laugh and exit the coach. "Very well," I say. "I'll walk with you."

He blinks at me, expression somewhere between amused and annoyed. "You're going to escort me to my hotel? Is that not a gentleman's duty for a lady?"

"Yes, but since you've so blatantly disregarded doing

so yourself, I'll have to show you how it's done." To the coachman, I say, "Drive on."

The coachman lifts his reins, but Albert holds up a finger to make him wait. The prince takes a step closer to me. "Don't you trust me?"

"No."

He clenches his jaw and taps his fingers against the curved silver top of his cane, reminding me of when he did the same over the backrest of the booth last night. This is the first time I've seen his jittery behavior all evening. Perhaps access to wine kept it at bay during dinner, and now my interference is keeping him from satisfying his craving.

I flourish a hand at the sidewalk. "Shall we?"

His fingers go still over his cane only to form a tight fist around it. "I wish you understood that you don't have to worry about me. I...I'm not who you think I am." He says the last part slowly, as if that will convince me.

While I do feel the slightest pinch of guilt over judging him, I don't know him well enough to trust that he won't reverse all the hard work we did tonight.

I lift my chin and meet his gaze with defiance. "I won't relent."

With a grumbling sigh, he runs a hand over his jaw. "You can't watch over me every minute of the day, you know."

The blood leaves my face at that. Not only is he right, but the thought of spending our married lives together with me constantly worrying over whether he'll ruin my reputation sends a surge of panic through me. Perhaps I should cut my losses while I can and find some other way to save my career...

"Very well," he says, gesturing toward the coach. "Let us ride back together. I'll escort you to your hotel like a proper gentleman."

"Oh, I don't think so." I step toward him, holding out my palm to halt him. At the same moment, he draws closer to usher me through the door. My palm collides with his chest, which makes us both freeze in place. Snatching my hand away, I draw in a sharp breath. Gathering my composure, I say, "We're walking. I want proof of this leisurely starlit stroll."

He pins me with a glower, and I realize this is the first time I've seen the carefree prince look so perturbed. Then, with exaggerated moves, he shuts the coach door and gestures for the coachman to drive on. "Fine, Miss Fairfield. Let us have a romantic walk."

As the coach rolls forward, Albert thrusts out his elbow—a silent request for me to take his arm. My pulse quickens at the thought of walking so close to him, but with the arrival of two couples exiting the restaurant, I know I have little choice. Taking my escort's arm while promenading is expected amongst human society, especially since my escort is my fiancé.

Pursing my lips, I sidle up next to Albert and place my hand at the crook of his elbow. Thankfully, my gloves and his jacket provide an adequate barrier between us. Perhaps he won't be able to tell how badly my hand trembles. I never used to get nervous about touching a man's arm. Or any part of him, for that matter. I relished every opportunity to get close to a suitor and often initiated such contact. Now...now, it's different. I feel more like an anxious girl entering society for the first time than a forty-two-year-old woman who's already experienced the ins and outs of a public courtship.

Albert tips his hat to the two couples as we stroll by. One of the women sinks into a curtsy, and—taking a cue from her—the others follow with curtsies and bows of their own.

Once our audience is out of earshot, Albert scoffs. "Your people have no idea how to treat me, do they?"

"What do you mean?" I ask, eager for a topic of conversation that will distract me from the prince's nearness.

"No one knows if they should bow or offer honorifics," he says without affront. It's more like amused curiosity. It makes me wonder if he's used to being overlooked, considering he's only one of his father's many sons. And a middle one, at that. "Not that your people owe a prince from another country such formalities."

"It's not just that," I say. "Faerwyvae holds different formalities than human-ruled countries. Only some of our fae kings and queens demand traditions of royal titles and genuflecting. Some prefer to avoid such conventions and only require respect."

"I can see that," he says. "Not even you have a royal title, correct? And you're the sister to the Unseelie Queen of Fire."

"Not even the husbands, wives, and mates of the fae royals are automatically given a title. It is up to each ruler to deem their partner a fellow king or queen. Either way, I didn't want a title. I get enough attention for being Evie's sister as it is. All I've wanted is renown for being myself."

"In other words, your career as a fashion designer?"

I glance over at him, surprised he's managed to glean

so much from my words, not to mention remembering what I said about the importance of my career in the first place. "Yes."

He lifts his cane and points it at my ensemble. "Is this one of your designs?"

"It is. I'll be wearing my work at each event we attend during our tour."

His lips twist into a sly grin. "Does that have anything to do with a certain scandal you mentioned last night? One that might have soured your reputation as a designer?"

My eyes narrow to slits, although a flutter of amusement tugs my lips. "You know, sometimes, you act far too keen for your own good. Is every prince in Bretton taught to read between the lines so adequately?"

He blinks a few times as if caught off guard. Then, tearing his gaze away, he takes on a more nonchalant bearing. "I assure you, my royal tutelage was far more boring than that. It's only that you're such a fascinating specimen. I'd be a fool not to analyze everything that escapes those lovely lips."

My breath hitches. There he goes with the false flattery again. This time, there's no one around to hear it, so it only serves to aggravate me. Just when I felt like we were reaching a safe and comfortable camaraderie too. I wonder if he shattered the mood on purpose, because it's certainly killed my interest in small talk.

We continue down the sidewalk in silence. The farther we get from the restaurant, the emptier the streets become. Here dark storefronts line the streets with only the occasional public house to break up the quiet monotony. My previous visits to the city of Jasper were during the day, so I didn't anticipate how inactive it gets after hours. Albert's hotel is still a couple blocks away, while mine is another block south from it—for I had the good sense to ensure our sleeping quarters were nowhere near each other—so we still have some ways to go.

We turn down another street darker than the others, with not even a tavern to interrupt the row of sleeping storefronts. The sight sends a chill down my spine.

"This is the leisurely path you meant to take?" I ask with a scoff. "If you weren't looking for some seedy pub, then I can't imagine why you wanted to walk back to your hotel. And alone, at that. You're a prince. Shouldn't you travel with guards?"

"I don't need guards," he says, tone somewhat distracted. His steps slow to a halt. "Although perhaps we should go down another..."

He glances over his shoulder only to abruptly proceed forward again. I nearly trip over my feet to keep up with his sudden stop and start. As we continue down the street, my heart begins to race, echoed by the rap of his cane against the sidewalk. I'm about to ask if he's trying to unnerve me when I notice his body listing to the side. Leaning heavily on his cane, his steps are now uneven, meandering.

"Why are you walking like that?"

He gives a sloppy shrug. "Darling, I think I had too much wine." His voice is too loud, his words too slurred.

I frown. "You hardly drank anything."

He glances over at me with a sideways grin. "That you know of."

"You had two glasses."

"Keeping track of my health, dearest? How sweet of you to watch me so carefully."

I open my mouth but can't reconcile this strange shift. He can't possibly be drunk. As often as I watched him swirl his glass and take long drinks from it, he only refilled it once. Each glass lasted far longer than I'd expect of a renowned drunkard. If we'd been served a fae variety of wine, then I could understand both the delayed effects and its potency. Which leaves only one explanation. This is all an act.

"Why do you do that?" I ask.

"Do what?"

I wave my free hand at him, gesturing from his cane and his stumbling feet to his irritating smile. "Keep changing from one persona to the next. One moment we're having a regular conversation. The next, you're saying something crass. Then, two seconds after that, you're about to fall on your face in an inebriated stupor."

"I wouldn't want you to get bored," he says with a wink. "We are to be married, aren't we? Until death do us part. That's a long time. Especially if rumors about aging in Faerwyvae are true. Are they? Will I stop aging now that I live here?"

While he's right about the rumors—humans on the isle do age slower, and those in close romantic relationships with the fae tend to age as slowly as their fae partners—I can't help feeling like he's trying to distract me. Even more telling is the way he appears to meet my gaze...only to shift his eyes slightly to the left, as if he's truly looking at something over my shoulder.

I'm about to turn around and see if there's some secret entrance to an underground vapor house that has him so transfixed, but he leans in close and whispers, "Keep your eyes forward."

"What are you—" Movement from up ahead has me swallowing my words. A figure emerges from the far end of the street and begins walking toward us. There's something sinister in the shadowed figure's slow, loping gait. Despite Albert's previous warning, I crane my neck to look behind us. There I spot two more silhouettes crowding in at the opposite end of the sidewalk. In a whisper, I hiss, "Albert!"

"I know," he mutters, then comes to a stumbling stop at the mouth of an alleyway. He raises his voice so it carries to our mysterious strangers. "Look, my dear! An alley. How quaint! Let's cut through."

As soon as we turn down the dark pathway, flanked by waste bins and the backsides of empty shops, Albert lowers his arm. My grip loosens from around his elbow, and he takes my hand instead. We jog down a ways but don't make it far before the slap of multiple footsteps approach the alley behind us. My heart slams against my ribs. "What's going on?"

Albert ignores my question and whirls me to face him. Before I realize what's happening, he closes in until my back comes against the wall of the nearest building. He stops before me, caging me in place with one hand propped beside my head, the other by my waist, still grasping the head of his cane.

I freeze as he leans closer, certain he's about to kiss me. Surely he can see this is hardly the time for a kiss. We're in danger, aren't we? The thought sends a strange thrill to my stomach, one I haven't felt since I embarked upon a mission of revenge against my first love. Back then, I delighted in danger. Relished every opportunity that could pit me against my enemy.

But...but that's not me anymore. And Albert should know better than to try to kiss me at all. Has he listened to nothing I've said? And yet, as I watch his mouth draw closer, I find myself unable to move. *Unwilling* to move. Instead, my eyes latch onto his mouth, taking in the sensuous curve of his bottom lip.

I plant both palms against his chest, unsure if I'm about to shove him away or pull him closer, but his lips don't come to mine. Instead, they draw next to my face. His breath stirs my hair. "As soon as I distract them, run."

The thrill in my belly goes still as good sense prevails over my moment of mind-boggling weakness. "What?"

He doesn't get the chance to explain. In the next moment, three male figures close in behind him and attack.

9

I t's too dark to see our assailants clearly, but it's obvious they mean us harm. Or Albert, at least. I stifle a shout as one of the men pulls the prince away from me and drives a fist into his abdomen. I flinch, expecting to see Albert heave forward, but it's his attacker who goes stumbling back. I note the way the man rubs his knuckles and how Albert has thrust out his cane.

The other two men close in. Albert grips his cane in two hands, one on the curved head, the other around the middle. Then, with a twist, a pointed blade emerges from the end.

Albert whirls toward one of the men and snaps his cane against the side of his face. As he falters, Albert turns to the other assailant and swings his weapon, slashing the bladed end through the man's throat. A spray of blood arcs into the air, splattering against one of the walls.

The first attacker rejoins the fray. Albert meets both men with a series of strikes, slashes, and punches, too fast for me to keep track of. All I can do is watch, my mouth agape, at the unexpected spectacle. The prince sends one man into a wall, where he's rendered unconscious as his head meets brick. The final assailant manages to grapple with Albert and bring him to the ground, but the prince rolls on top of him. In the next moment, he half rises and slams his cane blade into the other man's eye.

Albert remains in place, chest heaving, gaze locked on the man beneath him. My blood rushes through my ears, mingling with the frantic beat of my heart. It's so loud, I almost don't hear Albert when he speaks.

"You were supposed to run."

I don't know what to say to that. I'm too transfixed by the blood seeping across the stone floor of the alley beneath the man with the blade in his eye. My gut churns, half with disgust over what I'm seeing, half with shame that I didn't act.

I could have acted. I could have burned these men to a crisp. But...would that have been the right response? Who are they? What was their quarrel with Albert?

Shame takes over, making my shoulders hunch forward. Why would I even consider whether I should have joined the fight? I'm not a violent, vengeance-obsessed girl anymore. Besides, haven't I spilled enough blood in my past as it is?

"Why didn't you run?" Albert's tone is worn, edged with irritation. He rises to his feet and extracts the tip of his weapon from the man's eye. Like he did before, he twists the head of the cane. This time, the blade disappears. His eyes meet mine, and his expression softens. "I didn't want you to see this."

I take a steadying breath and force my tremulous

words past my lips. "I've seen worse." What I don't add is that I've done worse.

He frowns. "You have, haven't you?" Then, with a shake of his head, he returns his attention to the unmoving bodies and releases a long sigh. "We should go before anyone finds us. I'm pretty sure I killed them."

The way he says it so casually rouses me from my stupor. "You're pretty sure? The fact that you opened a man's throat and drove your hidden blade into another's skull didn't clue you in first?" I glance at the man slumped against the wall. Only now do I see the dark stain behind him where his head collided with brick.

"I thought they were fae," Albert says, stepping over one of the corpses to reach me. His tone is calm, calculated. Nothing like the slurring drunk he pretended to be before the attack. "I used excessive force. I would have held back if I knew they were human."

My mouth falls open, but I can't utter a word before he takes my elbow and tugs me away.

"We should indeed hurry, Miss Fairfield. I think we'd both like to avoid the papers for this little mishap."

I let him pull me a few steps forward before I wrench my arm from his grip. "What do you mean, you would have held back if you knew they were human? You used excessive force because you thought they'd be fae? What the bloody oak and ivy is that supposed to mean?"

"I expected our attackers to be fae because it makes sense that your kind would seek to assassinate a Brettonish prince."

"*My* kind? I'm human *and* fae, Albert, and you don't seem at all uneasy about taking the lives of either. Have you no concern over having killed three men?"

"Of course I do," he rushes to say, not hiding the ire in his tone. "Which is why I'd like to get us out of here as soon as possible."

I scoff. "You're concerned with getting caught for killing them, not over the act itself."

He holds up a finger. "First of all, these aren't the first men I've killed, so don't expect me to weep over their sorry corpses. Second, if you note the brass pin each of the men wear on their collars, you'll see they're Durrely Boys. Do you know who they are? A gang. Which means there are plenty more of them lurking around here somewhere."

I blink back at him. The Durrely Boys? I've only heard of the human gang in passing. They've never caused much trouble before. Not enough to garner the attention of the fae royals, at least. Although I admit I live a rather sheltered life when it comes to such matters.

"I'd prefer not to get my frock coat soaked with more blood. Wouldn't you say the same for that fabulous dress?" He says it all in a rush, his tone matching the aggravation in his eyes.

I take a step back from him. "What kind of prince are you?"

He purses his lips and begins tapping his foot in that anxious way of his. His fingers join in, drumming against the head of his cane. Now that I've begun to suspect his drunken behavior is an act, I'm less convinced that his occasional fidgeting is due to his craving for drink. "We really must go."

He reaches for me again, but I step back. "I'm not going anywhere with you until you tell me the truth. You're hiding something."

His tapping goes still, and he curls his hand tightly around his cane. "I do wish you'd simply believed me when I said I wasn't going drinking. Then you wouldn't be in this mess."

I shake my head, trying to piece together what he's saying. I recall the way he began limping and slurring just before the attackers closed in. He pretended to be weak, emboldening them to act. Then he countered their attack quickly. Efficiently. But what does that mean?

He pins me beneath his gaze and lowers his voice to a whisper. "You also should have believed me when I told you I'm not who you think I am."

My pulse quickens as his earlier words echo through my mind.

I wish you understood that you don't have to worry about me. I...I'm not who you think I am.

"What are you saying?"

He steps closer. "You asked me what kind of prince I am. The answer is I am no prince at all."

The blood leaves my face. "Then who are you?"

"My name is Dante. I'm a spy."

10

I nearly choke on the wave of shock that ripples through me. "A...a spy?"

"Yes, but you must believe me when I say I mean your nation no harm. I mean *you* no harm. My objective is to protect Prince Albert and ensuring the peace between our countries is genuine. Hence why I've made myself an easy target by acting like...like, well, the real Prince Albert."

I sway on my feet as realization dawns. The spectacle he made at the Salty Satyr, the drunken act in the street... it was all done to make himself appear vulnerable and attract potential threats.

He continues. "I was sent here to pose as the prince until his wedding day. If this marriage alliance proved to be a ruse to get revenge on King Grigory by assassinating his son, then I would intercept that danger and see that Albert was returned safely back to Bretton. If no threats to his life could be detected, then Albert would proceed with the wedding."

"So the real prince is here in Faerwyvae? Where is he? Was he the man I met at the pub?" I look at the prince— no, the spy—with dawning horror. "Are you wearing a disguise?"

"The answer is no to both questions. You've never met Albert. He remains safe back in Port Dellaray, protected by his guards."

A spike of rage heats my blood. "So you lied to me. You lied to me from the moment we met. Were you ever going to tell me you weren't Albert? Was I meant to find some unfamiliar man at the altar?"

"I would have told you eventually." He runs a hand over his face and begins tapping his foot in an agitated rhythm. Finally, he says, "I almost did. A few times. I wanted to, but if you had anything to do with a threat to Albert's life, I needed to keep my identity a secret from you as well."

I throw my hands in the air. "What about everyone else? Your face is plastered all over the broadsheets. Your face is the one society has seen. How were you planning to explain that?"

He releases a groan. "Can we please talk about this while we flee this corpse-strewn alley, at least? Or would you like to help me fend off a group of enraged Durrely Boys once they come looking for their comrades?"

My back stiffens as I'm reminded of the bodies littered behind me. "Fine," I say, marching forward. Before I can protest, he takes my hand and pulls me alongside him. With quick strides, we reach the mouth of the alley, opposite where we came in. The dark street that greets us reminds me of the danger we are likely still in. At least this time I know Albert—I mean, *Dante*—can take care of himself. And I'll have no qualms about using force too, even if it means conjuring the lethal fire magic I prefer to keep buried.

Dante looks both ways down the street, then hooks my hand around his elbow. In silence, we stroll to the next corner at a less conspicuous pace. A few figures approach, sending panic rising to my throat, but as they draw near, I see no sign of the brass pin the dead men were wearing or anything else to suggest that they're Durrely Boys. From the sway of their steps, I take it they've just come from drinking. Dante tips his hat like a proper gentleman, and I try to act as casual as I can. It takes all my restraint to keep the flurry of questions from bursting from my lips. We approach the next street, which—thank the All of All—is illuminated by an open tavern.

Just as we're about to reach the intersection, Dante turns me to face him. Framing my shoulders with his hands, he looks me up and down.

I shake myself from his grip. "What are you doing?"

"Looking for blood," he says, tone matter-of-fact.

"Blood?"

"You might have been spattered during the brawl, and I'd rather our ruffled state didn't give away the fact that we were just assaulted by a gang. Ah. There, on your chin."

I bite back a repulsed squeal and fling my gloved hand over my lower face, rubbing furiously. As I lower my hand, Dante shakes his head.

"Allow me." He takes a step closer, but I flinch back.

"I can do it myself." I rub my chin again, but Dante pulls my hand away.

"You're missing it completely. Hold still." This time, when he reaches for me, I freeze. He braces one hand gently on my shoulder and brings the tip of his gloved thumb to the corner of my mouth. Brow furrowed in concentration, he swipes his finger in soft strokes over my skin. He makes to step away, then shakes his head. "On your neck too."

"Disgusting," I say, wondering which of the dead men's blood now graces my flesh.

With clinical precision, Dante places a finger under my chin and angles my head to the side. Like he did with my chin, he begins to brush his fingers over the side of my neck. I inhale a sharp breath, my neck far more sensitive than my face. I try to hide my reaction by clearing my throat. "Are you going to answer my questions yet?"

He says nothing at first, just continues wiping at my neck. When he speaks, his voice is low. "I'm Prince Albert's decoy."

"His...decoy?"

"Every one of King Grigory's children has one, not to mention the king himself. I've served Bretton's military since I was a boy, and it wasn't long before I was recruited as Albert's decoy. We are not twins, of course, but we do have similar features. The same gold hair and blue eyes. Similar facial structure. No one who truly knew the prince would mistake us, but in public events where safety was required, I often stood in Albert's place."

He steps back and gives a nod to indicate he's finished.

"So your mission had you serving as his decoy since arriving here?" I ask.

"Yes, and while we never expected to fool you, we

fully intended to escape the detection of the press. Albert and I look similar enough that a few drunken photographs and in-person encounters with common pub-goers wouldn't reveal the truth. Like me, Albert cleans up well. It would be easy for unwitting strangers to believe we were one and the same."

It makes sense, I suppose. There's little chance the real prince would ever interact with those who saw Dante at the pub. And photographs—while far more damning than a simple sketch—can still be deceiving.

"What about the tour?" I ask.

He gives me a withering look. "Your tour certainly threw a wrench in our plans. Now check me over."

I frown, trying to reconcile the two statements. Then I realize the latter was a request for me to assess him the same way he did me. My eyes fall to his white shirt and tie, which are no longer white at all. I wrinkle my nose. "You're covered in blood."

As he works the knot in his tie, he casts a glance down the street, then at the pub. Two men loiter outside the doors, talking loudly, but they don't seem to notice us huddled at the corner. He removes his tie and begins loosening the buttons of his collar. "Albert declined your engagement tour at first because we knew it would complicate my mission."

"Then why did you—or he—agree to it when I came to the Salty Satyr?"

"Because I realized what a mess my actions had made for you. The apology I gave you was genuine. I never meant to harm your reputation with my mission." He finishes unbuttoning his shirt and asks, "Blood?"

My eyes widen when I take in how much of his chest

he's exposed. Although I suppose it suits the prince's reputedly rakish character. I point to the left side where his open collar remains saturated with evidence. He flips it this way and that, which does no good. With a roll of my eyes, I step forward and take matters into my own hands. My cheeks burn with heat as I tuck his filthy collar beneath his frock coat, which happens to give me a strong sense of the firm musculature beneath his flesh. Then, patting the collar in place, I say, "You're good now."

I lift my eyes to his and find his lips are curled into a smug smirk. "You've got quite nimble fingers," he says.

Flinching, I pull my hand from his torso. "I'm a dressmaker. Of course I have...nimble fingers." Why he found it necessary to comment upon them or flash me that stupid dimpled smirk is beyond me. Before I can think much of it, I whirl away from him and march around the corner.

He follows, keeping close to my side. "Do you wish to continue?"

"Continue what?" I say without looking at him.

"The engagement tour."

"And pretend everything is normal? Pretend I'm madly in love with a spy?"

"Is it much different from when you thought I was Albert?"

I halt in place and round on him. "Of course it's different. You lied to me. You broke my most important rule."

His brows knit together, and his vexing foot tapping commences. He purses his lips as if he wants to say something. Is that what his fidgeting conveys? That he's holding back from speaking? His foot goes still, and his smirk returns. "Technically, that rule was meant for your future husband. Which I am not."

I open my mouth to argue, but...he's right.

He's not my fiancé. He's not Albert, the man I'm meant to marry.

A strange sense of disappointment sinks my stomach, but it's soon replaced by the most profound relief.

"If you prefer, I can convince Albert to take his proper place," Dante says. "When I told him about our confrontation at the Salty Satyr and expressed how important the tour was to you, he still refused. He's too frightened to show himself in public until I've ascertained there is no threat to his life. Tonight's attack suggests such dangers are real, but not real enough for me to deem it an assassination attempt and have Albert call off the peace alliance. There's a chance we were simply in the wrong place at the wrong time. Either way, I must continue my mission. But I can look out for him in other ways. Tail him as a guard instead of acting as his decoy."

"You're saying my future husband is a coward?"

"To put it bluntly...I suppose you could say that. But he's also my friend. The closest thing I have to family."

I pull my head back with surprise. "The prince you serve is the closest thing you have to family?"

"I was orphaned as a child, before I can remember. My ticket out of the orphanage was joining the military. I was satisfied with that. Getting recruited as Albert's decoy, having a room at the palace, work that suited me... it was a luxury I never expected. Gaining Albert's friendship on top of that was more than I deserved."

I'm struck by a flash of sympathy, but it does little to endear me to Albert.

"The point is, he's a good man. He'll attend the tour if...if I strongly suggest it."

The grimace on his face says otherwise.

And yet, I find that oddly comforting. "So, Albert is a coward who has very little regard for me."

"That's not exactly—"

"He has no desire to see me before we're married. No desire to charm me or flirt with me or try to win my heart. I take it he isn't looking forward to marrying me at all."

"Again, that's putting it rather plainly."

"He's...not you. And everything you've been doing with me has all been an act. Your flirtations, your flatteries...you're just pretending to act like Prince Albert."

"I'm sorry, Miss Fairfield. If I thought I could tell you the truth without risking my mission, I would have done so right away. Now that you know the truth, you have every right to tell your sister and use it as grounds to sever your engagement. You could have me and Albert and all of his guards killed, and it would almost be justified. But if there's any part of you that wants peace and improved relations between our countries, I beg of you to keep this between us."

I'm surprised by his candor. His guilt. I could assuage some of his remorse by telling him he isn't the only one who was given a mission to test the validity of this peace alliance. My sister asked something similar of me—to spy on my betrothed and report on any suspicious activities. It's ironic, really. Maybe even humorous.

Something escapes my lips. A bark of laughter. Then another. Perhaps I've been overcome with a fit of mania in the wake of this evening's strange events, but as my relief grows, so too does my laughter.

"You and I are fake," I manage to say once I've somewhat sobered from my fit. "A temporary alliance before my union with the prince. We'll drink, we'll dance, we'll show society how madly in love we are, but then we'll go our separate ways. There will be no chance that either of us will mistake what we do together as something real."

"Yes," he says slowly, drawing out the word.

"This is perfect," I say under my breath, throwing my head back with a smile. "I'm so utterly relieved."

"Pardon?"

I chuckle again. A bundle of tightness unravels from my chest, making me feel lighter than I have since I first agreed to my marriage. Finding out the man I must spend my engagement tour with isn't my future husband is the best thing that could have happened. Now I can truly throw my efforts into this charade without having to worry about giving Albert the wrong impression. I'll still have to marry the prince, of course, and figure out how to act with him at public events when the time comes. But for now...

Now I get to relish in the comfort that this is all an act.

With a dreamy sigh, I draw close to Dante's side and place my hand at his elbow. My posture is loose, sultry, my muscle memory snapping into place as I take on a persona I discarded decades ago.

"Darling," I say, batting my lashes at the spy. His cheeks flush, which fills me with a long-forgotten sense of pride. "Take me back to my hotel. My feet ache, and I really must get my beauty sleep. We have many more social events to prepare for, you know."

His brow furrows as he stares down at me for a few silent moments. Then he dons that grin, one that surely has sent countless maidens swooning, and places his hand over mine. "Whatever you wish, my dearest." We proceed down the street, where another public house illuminates the sidewalk. Several patrons chat in front of the door. They go silent as we pass, but we keep our eyes locked on each other.

He leans closer, speaking loudly enough for his voice to carry. "Although I assure you, my love, you need no beauty rest at all. If you got any prettier you just might take my breath away."

"Oh, Albert," I croon in a sing-song voice, "you say the sweetest things."

11

Two days later, I bolt upright in my bed, awakened from a dream of blood. It makes sense that I would dream of such a morbid topic, after what happened in the alley. Those men were the first corpses I've witnessed since the war. Back then, gory nightmares were standard for me. I often woke screaming, unable to recall where I was. Sometimes not even *who* I was. Remembering my name was my only anchor to sanity, but even then, visions of death, of the lives Prince Cobalt forced me to end, plagued me.

I've had decades of healing to process such things. To end such horrid nightmares. I stopped dreaming of death after I came to terms with the things I did under compulsion. Forgiving myself for falling for the wrong man... now that is another story.

I'm not surprised I dreamed of blood. What I am surprised about is that it wasn't a nightmare. It may have started as one, with shadowed figures nipping at my heels, of alley walls closing in. But then Dante was there, spinning into action with his cane, much like he had in real life. A sense of safety came over me, and as soon as he spilled the first drop of blood, the dream shifted. The blood wasn't gory or terrifying but...beautiful. Something to be fascinated by. It became a trail of rubies littering bodies that weren't corpses at all but dress forms. I bent over, plucked a bloodred gem from the nearest faceless form, and marched out of the alley with Dante at my side.

I blink into the hazy morning light streaming through my curtains in my cottage bedroom, seeking any sign that I'm about to crash. That the blood and violence I conjured in my dream state will bring back unwanted memories. I'm aware that I should be disturbed by the dream itself, but I'm only shaken by my sudden jolt of wakefulness. No matter how long I sit and wait for the fear to take me, it doesn't. Instead, the final strain of thought I had in my dream grows stronger.

This would make the perfect button for my derby gown.

That's what held my fascination as I left the alley dreamscape. It was a glowing spark of inspiration.

A smile curls my lips and my limbs grow restless, desperate to move and get to my studio at once. Throwing back my blankets, I leave my strange dream behind and follow the pull it left instead. Because now I have a dress to alter.

AN HOUR LATER, I'M IN MY DOWNTOWN HAWTHORN studio, fixated on the gown in my lap. Three members of my design team have already arrived, but they don't pay me much mind. They know better than to interrupt me when I'm as frantic as I am now. I like to think of it as being one with my inner fire magic—my creative spark.

Who doesn't know better than to interrupt my state of urgent creativity, however, is Foxglove. "Amelie, I haven't seen you sew this fast since that one time you vowed not to use the toilet until you finished your sister's wedding veil."

I glance away from my work to cast a quick smile at my friend before I return my attention to the glittering ruby button I'm sewing in place. "Yes, well, I'm wearing this to the Zephyrus Derby tomorrow afternoon, and I only had the idea to change all the buttons from black to red this morning. I have to catch a train to the Wind Court tonight, and I have clients to see beforehand, so I must finish this soon."

He leans over my shoulder to assess my work. "Ah, the red certainly stands out against the black and white silk. And I do love how those rubies sparkle. It looks nice."

"It looks more than nice. It's perfect. I don't know how I didn't think of it before. I've had these ruby buttons just waiting to be used all this time..." I trail off and secure the thread, the tip of my tongue poking out at the corner of my mouth.

Foxglove says nothing in reply, and it takes me several beats to note the weight in his silence. I lift my gaze to his and find him grinning at me. "What is it?"

He pushes the bridge of his spectacles and gives a smug shake of his head. "Oh, nothing."

"Darling Foxglove, can't you see I'm busy?" I say it not with ire but a soft chuckle. "Take that ridiculous grin out of here or tell me what has you so amused."

He purses his lips to hide only a fraction of his growing smile and leans to the side until his elbow is propped on my worktable. "It's just...you seem inspired."

I give him a pointed look, then resume my work on the buttons. "Why do you think I'm sewing so fast? I'm in my creative spark."

"I do wonder, though. What's gotten you so inspired?"

His tone is suggestive, but I can't fathom what he's hinting at. Does he somehow know a bloody nighttime vision sparked my idea of ruby buttons? If so, I daresay he should be more mortified than smug.

He leans a little closer. "Or should I say...who."

Realization dawns, and my heart leaps so violently, I prick the tip of my finger with my sewing needle. I jolt at the sting but don't bother inspecting the wound. My fingers are used to such pricks and have the callouses to show for it. I already know for certain I didn't draw blood.

I pretend I didn't hear Foxglove and lower my brows as if I'm deep in concentration. The rustle of paper snags my attention. I hazard a glance at my friend just in time to see him extract a folded newspaper from his waistcoat. He clears his throat, and I avert my gaze.

"'Miss Amelie Fairfield and her brand-new beau, Prince Albert, were caught canoodling at the grand opening of the Golden Stone restaurant in Jasper, Earthen Court, this weekend. Prior to this, speculations had circulated over whether the couple was a true love match or merely a convenient ploy to help the fae fashion designer escape scandal. But after witnessing much hand holding and smoldering glances, it seems the match just may hold true adoration.'"

An unexpected blush rises to my cheeks, but I hide it

behind a casual laugh. "Foxglove, why are you acting like such good news is cause for pride? I told you about my engagement tour. I also told you that I have no feelings for my future husband."

"I know, I know," he says with a dismissive wave of his hand. "Just let me have my fun. Look how enamored you are!"

He turns the paper toward me, revealing a black-and-white sketch of what is meant to be Albert and me. His hand is clasped in both of mine, and I'm leaning so far over the table toward him, my breasts look as if they're a sneeze away from falling out of my bodice. Not only that, but they're twice as large as my real ones.

I snort a laugh. "It seems the reporter in attendance that night took many creative liberties."

"Oh, but you'll like this part. 'Miss Fairfield was dressed in a stunning evening gown that made her such a feast for the eyes, she nearly overshadowed the spectacular dishes served. The ensemble was doubtless one of her own designs, making it no surprise why she has risen so far in the world of fashion.'"

My heart leaps again, this time without an entry wound to accompany it. "The reporter really said that?"

"If I was going to make something up, it would be far cleverer than *a feast for the eyes*."

A surge of giddy joy ripples through me. I redouble my efforts on my current button, threading my needle into the cloth and through the eyelet at the back of the ruby bauble. "Then it's working. This engagement tour is really working."

"Yes, yes, but how was your first date? Did he kiss you?"

"Of course he didn't kiss me. We had dinner, he walked me back to my hotel, and we parted ways like any two strangers do. With a polite farewell." I'm leaving out quite a bit, primarily where we got ambushed by members of the Durrely Boys, but it really is the gist of what happened. We made it back to my hotel without any further issue, and Dante left to retire to his own lodgings. After learning the truth, I wasn't worried that he'd sneak off to a pub. If he wanted to court danger by skirting down dark alleys on his way to his hotel, that was fine by me, so long as I didn't have to be there.

"Very well. So your first date was boring. That can be expected. What about the prince himself? Tell me all about him. Is he handsome? Strong?" His voice deepens with no small amount of distaste. "Is he a drunken fool like you thought?"

I open my mouth, about to confess I don't know a thing about the real Prince Albert, but if I do that, I'll have to tell him about Dante. The attack. I trust Foxglove more than almost anyone. He's been one of my dearest friends ever since I was first given over as a bride to the fae. He was King Aspen's ambassador then, and the first kind soul I warmed up to.

So it isn't mistrust that has me holding my tongue. In fact, I'm not entirely sure why I don't just tell him. All I know is Dante went to great lengths to hide the truth of his mission. While I'm more concerned with salvaging my reputation than establishing formal peace and improved trade with Bretton, it feels wrong to share secrets not even I should have been privy to.

"The prince," I say as I tie off the thread securing yet

another button, "is not as bad as I thought. He's...adequate."

"Adequate?" Foxglove's tone is icier than if I'd said seven doilies is more than enough to decorate a room. "*Adequate*? That's all you have to say about him?"

I shrug and reach for a new button. "What did you expect?"

He pushes off from my worktable and throws his hands in the air. "Oh, I don't know. Maybe that he smells like moonlight or is hung like a centaur. *Something*. I've given you all the juicy details about Fehr. It's what friends do."

"You know I'm the worst friend for such gossip. I'm not very...active in such exploits. And I assure you, I have no intention of doing any of that with my husband."

Foxglove falls into another stretch of silence, and I get the sneaking suspicion he's smirking again. Finally, he mutters, "We'll see about that."

I pause, my needle halfway through the silk sleeve of the gown. "What's that supposed to mean?"

He nods at the dress in my lap. "Like I said, Amelie. *Inspired*. Love will do that, trust me." With a fluttering wave, he takes his leave and heads for the staircase that will take him down to his studio's floor. I gape after him, indignation writhing through me, battling with my need to argue my case.

I'm not inspired out of love for my fiancé. And certainly not because of Dante. I'm inspired because of some strange dream. Sure, Dante was in that dream, but the creative spark didn't come from him. Well, the blood came from him. Or his actions, more like. And I admit his presence made me feel safe enough to realize the blood was actually rubies, but...but it was a damn dream. Not reality.

I shake my head with a scoff and return to my stitches. Foxglove can think whatever he likes. I know my own heart. There's no way—not a single chance—that I'll ever fall in love with my husband.

12

W hen Dante picks me up from the train station for our next date the following afternoon, it isn't in a coach-and-four but a mechanical beast with an insufferable roar.

"Do you like it?" he says as he steps out of the boxy black automobile and takes my luggage bag from me. The driver tries to leave the front seat to take Dante's place, but the spy waves at the older man, gesturing for him to remain behind the wheel.

Dante tucks my bag in the storage compartment at the back of the car while I assess the metal beast with a wrinkled nose. Focusing on the automobile and not Dante—dressed in yet another elegant suit, dark blue this time—helps distract me from the strange way my heart kicks up at being in his presence again. My chest has been acting funny all day, bubbling with something akin to excitement whenever I was reminded of our approaching second date. I know it's only because I'm thrilled to be showing off today's ensemble, replete with my newly sewn ruby buttons running down the sleeves and back of the dress. And perhaps I am a little pleased about seeing Dante himself, mostly because of the relief our mutual ruse has brought me.

I shake my head at the car and take the gloved hand Dante proffers to help me into the vehicle. A warm tingle runs over my palm at his steady touch. It's then I realize I haven't answered his question. "I've only ridden in an automobile a time or two, and I can't say I care for them much."

He chuckles as I climb inside and take a seat. The *only* seat, I note, aside from the one the driver occupies. Which means Dante must sit right next to me. I try to scoot toward the opposite door to give him more room, but my layered skirts and the wide brim of my hat prevent me from getting too far.

"Why don't you like automobiles?" he asks as he settles in beside me and closes the door.

As the driver sets the vehicle rolling forward, a sense of vertigo comes over me. I close my eyes and fling my arms out to the sides, seeking any kind of handhold. One of my gloved hands comes to the closed door, while the other is suddenly caught in a strong grasp. Opening my eyes, I find Dante grinning over at me, my hand clasped in his.

Heat rises to my cheeks as I—as calmly as I can—extract my palm from its temporary refuge and place both hands in my lap instead. Then, scowling at Dante, I say, "I dislike cars because they're unnecessary and vile."

His grin widens. "Oh, come on. It can't be much different from a horse-drawn carriage."

I lift a finger and begin ticking them off one by one.

"They're louder, smellier, and scarier. And they make me dizzy."

"What about trains? Considering the station I just picked you up from, you have no qualms with them."

"I don't like trains much either, but they are necessary for swift travel. Cars, on the other hand, are just redundant."

He lets out an exaggerated gasp. "How could you say that? She'll hear you."

I quirk a brow. "She?"

"Yes," he says, running an affectionate hand over the seat. "I think I'll call her Bertha."

"She isn't...yours, is she? Please don't tell me you bought this monstrosity."

He releases a heavy sigh. "Unfortunately, Bertha is Albert's baby now. And yours too, I suppose, once you marry him. Shared assets, and all that. It was literally Albert's first request upon arriving on the isle. When he saw that carriages still outnumber automobiles here, he demanded I purchase a car in his name so he can ride around *in style* once he resumes his proper place."

I cast a glance at the driver. Unlike in a coach, the man operating the vehicle sits only a few feet in front of us, so I have no doubts that he can hear our conversation.

Dante must read the concern in my eyes. "Digby is with us. He's one of the prince's guards, so he knows everything. Including the fact that you now know the truth."

"Ah." For some reason, a delighted thrill runs through me at how he says *with us*, reminding me that I'm one of the very few people who know about his mission. Not only that, but Dante trusted me enough to inform others that I've been let in on the secret. A smile begins to form on my lips, so I hide it behind a question. "Do you mean to say automobiles outnumber carriages in Bretton?"

He nods. "They have for several years now. Bretton is number one when it comes to vehicle manufacture. It makes sense that Faerwyvae is behind in that regard, considering the minimal trade between our two countries. After your marriage to the prince, you might see more baby Berthas rolling down the streets."

"Great," I mutter, placing a hand over my churning stomach. I glance out the window to see if it will steady my nausea. Flat green fields extend out in every direction, with only a few sparse hills in the distance. Today's public outing for me and the false prince is the Zephyrus Derby, the most popular race in all of Faerwyvae. It's held at Galewood Downs in the countryside about an hour from the train station we just departed from. People travel from all over the isle to the Wind Court in anticipation of the occasion, which makes it the perfect place to show off my dress and my feigned premarital bliss.

"You look stunning, by the way." Dante's eyes rove from the hem of my black-and-white striped skirt to the asymmetrical gathered waist, then rest briefly on the deep V-neck bodice. He flicks his gaze to mine, and a flush of color darkens his cheeks.

Did I just...fluster him with my mere hint of cleavage? If he were anyone else, I'd slump my shoulders, turn away, or do anything to rebuff what might be a sign of budding attraction. But he's not anyone else. He's a spy. An actor. Even if he truly did find my feminine assets pleasing for a spare moment, it doesn't matter because we both know what our arrangement is. It's temporary. Fake. Safe.

So instead of doing what I might have done with any other hot-blooded male, I sit a little taller, letting my chest lift even higher, and flourish the cuff of my ruched silk sleeves. "Do you like my buttons? I sewed them on last minute."

"They're lovely. Although you should have used emeralds instead. They'd bring out your eyes."

I huff a laugh and try not to read too much into the way my heart gives a dainty flutter.

"I suppose it doesn't matter if you tried to bring out your eyes," he says, sliding his gaze to the top of my head, "for that is a very large hat."

"Why, thank you," I say, giving the brim an affectionate pat, much like he did the seat of the car.

His lips curl into a smirk. "I didn't realize that was a compliment."

I lift my chin and give him a knowing look. "It is where we're going."

At the end of our hour-long journey, the driver pulls up before the main entrance to Galewood Downs amongst the coaches and even a few other automobiles. This time Dante allows Mr. Digby to open the door for us, as befitting a prince. As we exit, my eyes fall on the cane Dante once again carries. I can't help being reminded of the alley and the impressive way he turned the stick into a weapon, even before he revealed its hidden blade. Hopefully, he'll have no reason to use the cane in such a way today.

Dozens of other parties exit their vehicles or stroll up the steps to the front doors. A wave of anxiety washes over me in anticipation of mingling amongst society for only the second time since the scandal struck, and this event is far more social than a quaint dinner at a new restaurant. As soon as Dante offers his arm and gives me a reassuring wink, my nerves settle. As long as I'm seen at my prince's side, there will be no room for scandal in others' minds. Especially with how sharp my escort looks today. I admit he makes for a delectable piece of eye candy, with his crystal blue eyes, lean figure, and sun-kissed golden hair. It's then I realize this is my first time seeing the spy in full daylight. Our first two encounters were at night, cast in shadows and dim electric bulbs.

"Shall we?" He gestures with his still-waiting arm, making me realize I've yet to take it.

I place my hand at his elbow, and we join the flow of foot traffic into the main building. Beyond the front doors is a flurry of activity, with lines of people stretching before the betting windows and concession stands.

"Care for any refreshments, dearest?" Dante asks.

"No, my love, let us claim our seats first."

We bypass the lines and make our way to the back of the building where it opens to the stands. Several bays of tiered seating sprawl out on both sides, extending toward the track. To the far right of the stands is a plush lawn where a large white tent is perched. That must be Queen Ilma's tent. Anyone of importance will be there, mingling with the other members of the upper crust. Ilma is the Seelie Queen of the Wind Court, a monarch I'm not personally acquainted with. My sister knows her well enough, I'm sure, but I've never been introduced to her. Still, I can't help but stare at the tent with no small amount of longing. Do I dare be so presumptuous as to enter it uninvited?

"I see what you mean about large hats, Miss Fairfield." With his cane tucked under his arm, Dante gestures at the stands, then at the lawn outside the queen's tent. Countless well-dressed women wear hats as large as mine, decorated with silk flowers, feathers, and even a stuffed bird or two.

I give him a sly look. "Told you."

"Miss Fairfield, I'm surprised to see you here." A nasally feminine voice has my gut dropping to my feet as Lydia Mangrove approaches us, arm-in-arm with a mustached gentleman.

"Miss Mangrove," I say, unable to hide my terse tone. And why should I? Lydia made herself my nemesis by tricking me into taking Mr. Vance's measurements at the fashion showcase.

She turns her gaze to my companion and offers a quick curtsy. "This must be the Brettonish Prince you're reputedly engaged to. So sudden! Why is that, Miss Fairfield? You seemed rather...unattached at the fashion showcase."

"If I seemed that way to you, Miss Mangrove, then I daresay you might be a bit obtuse."

Dante snorts a laugh but hides it behind an attempt to clear his throat.

Lydia ignores my jab and gives my ensemble an unimpressed once-over. "Speaking of the showcase, isn't that one of the dresses you brought along? You know, before you were banned from presenting your line?" She says each word with feigned innocence, which grates on my nerves a thousand times more than if she'd expressed her disdain plainly.

Of course, two can play at her game. With a wide grin, I sweep my hand over my skirt, smoothing the pleated folds and angling my wrist so the ruby buttons catch the sunlight. "It is. Some of my best work, if I say so myself."

She scoffs. "Don't tell me you plan on turning social events into your own personal fashion show."

"Why? Are you not doing the same?" I cock my head, then assess her gown. It's a pretty linen day dress that suits her frame nicely, but I won't tell her that. Instead, I give her a somber shake of my head. "No, I can clearly see you aren't. Perhaps if you dressed better in public you'd have a bevy of clients and wouldn't have to resort to petty sabotage."

Lydia blinks several times, her face paling before it begins to darken into a crimson hue. She clearly didn't expect me to discard our little game in favor of more direct barbs.

I shift my gaze to Dante, leaning into him until our shoulders brush, and speak in a loud whisper. "My dear, let us adjourn to Queen Ilma's tent. I'm not impressed with the company we'd have to keep in the stands."

Lydia makes a mortified squeak in the back of her throat, mouth gaping open.

"Enjoy the races, Miss Mangrove," I say with a curt nod. She's still sputtering wordlessly as Dante and I brush past her and her wide-eyed escort. A spark of pride ignites in my chest, flooding me with the most delectable sense of victory.

We hardly make it five steps before I feel Dante heaving with a quiet chuckle beside me. "Oh, Amelie."

Perhaps I'm just riding the high of my triumph, but the way he says my name, voice strangled with suppressed laughter, has my stomach tightening. My mind goes to the strangest, most inappropriate place, and I find myself curious over what *Oh, Amelie* would sound like in a different circumstance. One that didn't involve clothes.

I shake the thought from my head. Why would I wonder such a thing? It's surely been too long since I last attended to my...urges. Knowing Dante isn't the real prince must have informed my subconscious mind that he's fair game. A valid candidate for the meaningless trysts I occasionally partake in with a willing partner. That's the only explanation I can think of. Whatever the case, I cannot sully our working relationship with such fleeting fancies. Or...can I?

Dante's eyes bore into my profile, and I hope he can't see my vulgar musings written across my face. "I knew your tongue was sharp," he says, still chuckling, "but in truth, you are simply wicked."

I scowl at him, ready to berate him for making fun of me, but those damn dimples of his have me tongue-tied.

He holds up his free hand. "I mean it in the best way, dearest. Do you recall what I said the day we met?" He lowers his voice and brings his lips as close to my face as my hat will allow. "I like a woman with a little fire."

13

My first glimpse of the queen has my feet rooted in place. We're still several paces from the tent, but her imposing figure stands out amongst the aristocrats swarming about inside. Queen Ilma sits on a thronelike chair, flanked by well-dressed female attendants—all human, from the looks of them, much like the guests who fill the tent. Behind the queen, a pair of blue feathered wings span out on either side of her chair. It's the only visual evidence that she's a bluebird fae. From what I know, she rarely shifts into her bluebird form and prefers to remain humanoid.

My gaze falls on her gown, and I nearly choke on my own admiration. It's a confection of white brocade, abundant ruffles, and pale blue lace. The square neckline of the bodice and extra wide skirt evokes a style once popular amongst human royals a few decades past. Her silver hair is done up in an outrageously large coiffure that puts my oversized hat to shame. Sapphires and pearls sparkle at her ears from their lobes to their pointed tips, while her neck is adorned in diamonds and a blue crystal pendant the size of a chicken egg.

My gown and ruby buttons no longer feel quite so stunning. Even less so now that sweat has begun pooling beneath my armpits. Why did I come here? I felt bold when I declared to Lydia Mangrove that I would visit the queen, but now...now I feel like an impostor. What right do I have to be here? My career may be well known amongst the fae, but considering the human style of Ilma's gown—not to mention the mostly human company she appears to keep—my work is likely unknown to her.

"Come, my love," Dante says, taking a step toward the gaping maw of the tent. With my hand still tucked at his elbow, it forces me to take a step too.

A man in a black suit and white bow tie intercepts us. He's full fae, as told by his pointed ears and pale blue hair, and appears to be one of the few pureblood fae figures in the tent, aside from the queen. As he stares down his nose at us, I realize he must be the queen's butler. "Invitation?"

I open my mouth but not a sound comes out. While I assumed only elite members of society could enter the tent, I didn't anticipate a need for formal invitations.

Dante, unflustered by the request, says, "I'm Prince Albert, son of King Grigory of Bretton. This is my fiancée, Miss Amelie Fairfield, sister to Queen Evelyn of Fire. As this is my first time in the Wind Court, I would like to pay my respects to Queen Ilma."

He says it with such poise and regal confidence that it's no wonder he was recruited as the prince's decoy.

The butler's eyes flash from Dante to me and back again. Then, wordlessly, he scurries into the tent and approaches the queen. He whispers something to her, and Ilma's gaze slides to us. I try to evoke some of Dante's confidence, but the frantic pulse of my heart sends my knees quivering.

"Don't be nervous," Dante whispers.

"I'm not nervous," I bite back, grateful I can lie.

The queen cocks her head, and her butler whispers something else. A bright light flashes somewhere inside the tent, and I realize—with no small amount of horror—that there are reporters and photographers inside. I knew they would likely document today's event, but how could I have failed to foresee that they would be in the queen's tent too? If I'm rejected from her audience and the moment is captured by pen or film...

"She'll love you, Amelie," Dante says, patting the hand clenching tighter and tighter around the crook of his elbow. When I fail to acknowledge his attempt at reassurance, he adds, "If not for your personality, then certainly for that gorgeous swell of breasts you have on display."

I'm so shocked by his words that I can't help but wrench my gaze from the queen to stare at Dante. "Excuse me?"

A sly grin plays around his lips. "I mean, look at Her Majesty. Her own breasts seem to defy gravity, the way they sit horizontal like two steamed buns on a platter. How could she not be impressed by what you've done with your own?"

His eyes dip down to my décolletage, drinking me in with exaggerated approval. I belatedly steel my expression into one of affront. It's all I can do to hide the blush that heats my cheeks. Even so, I feel my countenance cracking at the edges, filling with amusement. I playfully swat his arm. "You are being rather crass, Your Highness."

"I'd like to think I'm simply being honest." Like some storybook rogue, he slowly drags his tongue over his lower lip, which somehow comes across as both seductive and ridiculous. I nearly burst out laughing.

A throat clears before us and I find the queen's butler has returned. It's then I note how my angst has dissipated, melted into a pool of ease during Dante's vulgar observations. Did he do that on purpose? Distract me because he sensed my growing distress?

"The queen will see you now," the butler says, gesturing for us to enter the tent.

OUR INTRODUCTION TO THE QUEEN GOES FAR MORE smoothly than I anticipated. She's civil, if not a little terse, and seems rather fascinated with the false Prince Albert. Considering Albert is the son of the man who once attempted to annihilate the isle and every living creature on it, I'm surprised by her interest. She asks him about automobiles, food, and the latest fashions in Bretton. It reminds me that there have always been fae who find humankind intriguing. It's why fae learned to shift into seelie form in the first place, eager to resemble their source of fascination.

Once Ilma is satisfied with news from Bretton, she turns her attention to me.

"Miss Amelie Fairfield," she says, her voice light and

airy. Appropriate for the Seelie Queen of the Wind Court. "Queen Evelyn is your sister, correct?"

"Yes, she is," I say, trying my best to act proud of the fact rather than irked at not being known foremost by my career. But this is good, isn't it? She might not have agreed to meet me if not for my royal relation to Evie.

"Your sister is quite famous," she says. "The queen who started and ended a war."

"Yes, that's her," I say, grateful that my involvement in said war is lesser known. If she was aware that my lust for my sister's fiancé was used to pave the path toward political upheaval, she'd be undoubtedly less warm to me now.

"But you're somewhat renowned yourself, aren't you Miss Fairfield?"

My heart leaps into my throat. Was I wrong? Does she know the truth? Evie has always done her best to protect me and hide the more painful details of my past, but...oh no. What if she means my recent scandal?

"I always considered your fashions too fae for my tastes," the queen says.

"My fashions," I echo. Relief washes over me.

"I prefer human designs." She gestures at her immaculate gown. "Especially ones modeled after history. You should do more of that."

I'm so stunned that she's talking about my work—not the war, not the scandal—that I almost can't summon my reply. Finally, I manage, "That's a lovely idea, Your Majesty."

She lifts her chin and assesses my ensemble. "Are you wearing one of your own designs now?"

"I am."

"Hmm."

I can't tell whether she made the sound out of approval or distaste, so I say nothing.

"As you can see," Dante says, "my fiancée does a wonderful job at designing after human sensibilities as well. This dress she wears now would have my mother emptying the royal coffers at once. But not before locking Miss Fairfield into an exclusive contract as her royal dressmaker."

Queen Ilma's eyes go wide, and she assesses my dress with renewed fascination. "You truly think Queen Mary would covet such a gown?"

"I do. Were my fiancée in Bretton, she'd be the wealthiest fashion designer around." He releases an exaggerated sigh and casts an adoring gaze upon me. "If only those in Faerwyvae would catch up with Brettonish style and see what a prize my darling Amelie is."

Ilma flutters an apologetic hand at my companion. "We have been known to be behind the latest trends here, Prince Albert. And you're right." She turns her gaze to me. Or my dress, more like. "This gown is perfection."

I can't stop the grin from stretching over my lips, despite how my mind tries to tell me I didn't truly earn the compliment. It was gained more through careful coercion on Dante's part than genuine appreciation of my work. "Thank you, Your Majesty. You're too kind."

"You must design a dress for me, Miss Fairfield."

My heart jumps so hard, I fear it will tumble out of my ribcage. "Of course, Your Majesty. I would be honored."

A bright light flashes to my right. From my periphery, I notice a photographer eagerly watching my interaction with the queen. I stretch my smile wider just as he takes the next photograph. Behind him stand two reporters, scrawling in their notebooks. For once, I'm gleeful over their presence. *Please, document away, you troublesome menaces.*

"Give your contact information to my butler," the queen says, then gives us a magnanimous nod—a clear dismissal of our company. As we leave the queen's audience, I feel as if I'm floating on air. I'm so pleased, I almost forget to speak with her royal butler. Thankfully, Dante guides us over to him where I relay the queen's request and deliver my contact information.

Afterward, I'm too ecstatic to remain in the tent. Not even the ornate spread of tea, wine, and tiny confections can tempt me to stay. Perhaps I'm also a little worried I might ruin a perfect interaction if I overstay my welcome. Instead, Dante and I take our places before the fence that lines the track. We remain in view of the royal tent, a clear signal to those in the stands that we belong amongst the aristocrats. After meeting the queen, I might even believe it's true.

There is one thing, though, that nags the back of my mind.

I cast a glance around, ensuring no one is close enough to overhear. The first race has yet to begin, so the fence line has yet to grow too crowded. I edge closer to Dante.

"You didn't have to lie to the queen for me," I say, keeping my voice low.

"It wasn't much of a lie," he says. "Albert's mother would love your gown. The funny thing is, while many in Faerwyvae seem obsessed with Brettonish fashion, there are plenty in Bretton who seek a fae flair to their wardrobe.

I lift my brows. "Truly? Even with the discord between our countries?"

"Even so. Not everyone believes Faerwyvae is nothing but a wild wasteland full of monstrous baby-stealing creatures with gnashing teeth."

"I suppose that's good to know. Still, I don't need you to rescue me. I appreciate what you did, but from now on, please note that it's important to me that I build my career based on my own merits."

His tone turns somber. "I apologize if I overstepped my bounds."

I release a sigh. "I'm not upset."

"Good," he says, patting my gloved hand, still at his elbow. He doesn't release it though. Instead, he rests his palm on the back of my hand. "Besides, you don't have to worry about me rescuing you much longer. In ten days, you'll be marrying the real Albert."

An icy chill runs through me. Ten more days until my wedding? How did it come so soon?

Dante's lips spread wide, but his grin doesn't reach his eyes. "After that, our ruse will be over. It will be him at your side, not me."

Am I imagining the note of disappointment in his voice? Does it have anything to do with how my gut sinks at his words?

A tapping sound fills my ears, and I note the way he drums his free hand, fingers fluttering, on the head of his cane. In the next instant, his hand goes still and he averts his gaze toward the track.

"Trust me," he says, his tone so jovial it makes me

certain I was indeed mistaken when I thought I sensed a hint of gloom in his mood. "The real Albert won't even consider treating you like a damsel in distress when it comes to your career. He has a terrible sense of fashion."

I chuckle, but I'm all too aware of the tightening of my chest. I may have imagined his momentary disappointment when he mentioned the end of our arrangement, but I can't help wondering...did I imagine my own?

14

The fence line grows a little more crowded as the first race begins, but Dante and I manage to maintain some semblance of privacy. It seems those on the lawn—in other words, those worthy of standing within eyesight of the queen—know better than to lose their composure right now. The clusters of couples and small groups joining us near the fence keep their distance from us and others, daring not to crowd in too close or act overeager. The racers may be on display for us, but we are on display for the queen.

Half a dozen sleek black equine creatures race past us on the track, sending up a gust of wind in their wake. The brim of my hat flutters but the ample pins I secured it with ensure it doesn't go flying off my head.

Dante stares after the pucas, mouth hanging on its hinge. "I've never seen something run so fast."

"Just wait until you see the kelpies."

His gaze shoots to mine. "Kelpies? You mean those

man-eating horses that like to drown their victims before they tear them apart with razor-sharp fangs?"

I grimace because—unlike most other tales about the fae—he isn't wrong. "Kelpies have a bad reputation, and some do still try to eat people, but they aren't all monstrous. Some are rather nice. In fact, my sister is good friends with one. She had to feed him a human to gain his trust and admiration. In her defense, the human she fed him was a vile man."

Dante pales, expression uncertain. "Are you teasing me right now?"

I'm not, only exaggerating slightly, but he doesn't need to know that. My only response is a tight-lipped smile.

A cheer roars through the stands as the fastest puca crosses the finish line.

Dante tucks his cane under his arm and brings his hands together in polite applause. "Are all the racers fae? I haven't seen a single rider, only creatures."

"Yes. All are fae and race on their own without a rider controlling them."

"I had no idea we weren't just going to a simple horse race," he says. "Is there such a thing as a simple horse race on the isle?"

"Hardly. Why bet on horses when you can bet on far faster creatures?"

He furrows his brow and casts a glance around the lawn and stands. "This derby...it's mostly a human event, isn't it? Humans watching fae creatures race and betting on the results?"

I nod. "All our dates on this tour are human events."

He lowers his tone, but there still isn't anyone close

enough to hear us. "Because you seek to grow your career in the human market."

"Yes," I say, once again surprised at how well he remembers the things I tell him. I suppose it's a spy's job to gather intel and easily recall it.

The furrow between his brow deepens.

"What is it?"

Another group of puca begin the next race, speeding along the track with preternatural grace.

Dante follows the creatures' progress with his eyes. He leans closer. "It's just...fae creatures are more sentient than regular animals. They're people, aren't they?"

I'm taken aback by the concern in his expression. "That's strange coming from you. Despite you saying not everyone in Bretton thinks the fae are monsters, I seem to recall you exclaiming my lack of fangs and claws when we first met."

He chuckles. "I was merely playing a part."

"You're saying the real Prince Albert would have responded that way?"

Dante gives a dismissive shrug. Another roar of cheers erupts as the second race ends.

"So my future husband is a buffoon," I mutter, not intending for my voice to reach Dante's ears.

No such luck.

He angles his head toward me. "Don't be too hard on the prince. I admit I too held many uninformed assumptions about faekind, long ago. But as a spy, I've gathered much intel about your isle. Being here now, even after such a short time, has taught me much more. He too will learn to see Faerwyvae the way I do. I'm sure of it."

My muscles coil tight, and a sudden urge to fidget

comes over me. My future with Albert is the last thing I want to talk about. So I turn the subject on him. "What's your surname? I feel like I should know a little more about you. It's only fair, considering you've likely gathered infinite intel on me."

He hesitates before answering. "I don't have a surname."

"Why not?"

"My parents died in a plague that swept Bretton when I was still a baby. I was one of many children brought to the orphanage at the same time. We were lucky to have a roof over our heads. Beds. People to feed us. The nurses and caretakers did their best, but keeping records of every orphaned child's parentage was simply not manageable at the height of the plague."

Despite how he keeps his tone light, I see the way his lips turn down, eyes losing some of their jovial spark.

"I'm sorry, Dante," I whisper. Before I can stop myself, I add, "I lost my mother during the war. So...so I know..." A lump sears my throat, and I swallow it down.

"That must have been hard."

I force a smile. "It was, but enough about that. How did we get on such a dreary topic?"

He watches me in silence for a few moments, ignoring the final race between the puca, while I pretend to be engrossed in discovering the victor. Why did I have to bring up Mother? Dante doesn't need to know about the pains in my past. He's a temporary ally, not a friend.

Dante finally tears his gaze from me, just as another race begins. This time, moon mares race down the track. His eyes widen as the skeletal horses gallop past us. "What the hell are those?"

"Moon mares," I say, relieved that our conversation has ebbed back into safer waters. "They reside primarily in the Lunar Court. Despite their frightening appearance, they're rumored to be well-mannered."

"Intriguing." He rubs his jaw, and a curious expression crosses his face. "Is it true all fae have two different physical forms? Seelie and Unseelie?"

"It's true, although not all fae choose to shift."

"Can only pureblood fae shift?"

"No, but it is often easier for them to learn how to than those of us with only some fae blood."

He looks me over. "Can you shift?"

A flutter of panic strikes me. "I never have," I say, evading any mention that I probably could if I wanted to. It's the same issue as my magic—part of me is afraid of my fae powers. Ashamed of them. Using the element of fire to generate creativity is a beautiful expression. Creating flame, on the other hand, comes from a much darker place inside me. I fear shifting forms would come from the same rage and hatred my flame springs from.

"My sister can shift though," I rush to say, diverting the topic from me. "Her unseelie form is a fox."

"A fox?"

"Yes, a little white fox covered in pink, blue, and purple flame. She's very cute, but never say that to her face. Nor should you try to pet her. She bites."

His chest heaves with laughter. "I'll have to pass the warning on to Albert. He's more likely to meet her than I am, I presume."

My stomach drops at yet another reminder that our ruse will soon come to an end. I was so relieved when I learned Dante would only be a temporary fixture in my life, but I underestimated how comfortable I'd feel around him. I was comfortable enough to bring up my mother, after all. I'm sure most of that ease comes from the fact that Dante will undoubtedly leave. That he poses no threat to my heart. However, there's a small part of me that recognizes the hidden lie. The truth is, I'm comfortable around Dante because...because he's *him*. He's easy to talk to. Easy to touch and be physically close to without being reminded of dark memories, of a time when touch was forced upon me under the haze of compulsory fae magic. I could tell myself I'd feel the same around any temporary ally, but I can imagine a hundred other men I'd be miserable around were I playing this charade with them.

It takes me a moment to realize Dante is still talking. I blink a few times to rid myself of my prior train of thought and focus on his words.

"He's known for making an ass of himself around animals when deep in drink. He once got so drunk on a hunt that he wandered off and woke up in a den of wild boars." He looks over at me, and the mirth drains from his face. "Not that your sister is an animal. That's not what I meant."

I realize my expression must have shifted with my thoughts, so I force a smile. "No, of course you didn't."

His smile returns. "Albert, though, he is an animal."

Another moon mare race begins. The previous one must have ended while I was lost in my musings. Musings I shouldn't have had in the first place. What's wrong with me? Why am I suddenly acting like our companionship is real? This is all an act. His attention. Our easy touch. Even his persona. The Dante I know is entirely fabricated, and I would do well to remember that.

"So that story was true," I say. "The one you were telling at the pub."

His dimples deepen. "I may have exaggerated a bit, but yes. Your beloved prince is known to get himself into many a funny situation. You won't be short on entertainment with him."

Clenching my jaw, I focus on the track, watching the moon mares speed toward the finish line. "I don't need entertainment. I need a husband who won't embarrass me."

He angles his body closer, and I can tell he wants me to look at him. But I can't. "He won't, Amelie. I've delivered your terms, your ground rules. Told him what you need from your marriage. He may be...a bit of a character, but he's a good man. The kindest of all King Grigory's children. He befriended me when he could have simply treated me like any other guard, spy, or royal decoy."

I lift my chin, unimpressed with his praise.

"I apologize if I've made him sound foolish. That was never my intention. You'll like him well enough." From the corner of my eye, I catch him worrying his lower lip. Then, lowering his voice further, he adds, "Perhaps more than like."

I scoff. "No. That's an impossibility."

He studies my face, blue eyes turning down at the corners. "Why? Why are you so certain you won't love him?"

"Because," I say, keeping my voice level, "I don't want to love him. Or anyone else."

"Why?"

"Love has never been kind to me." I try to keep my voice firm, but it comes out with a tremor. "And I have been far too kind to it, much to my detriment. I will not play that game again."

"Who hurt you?" His voice is shockingly cold, a quaver of restraint rippling through it.

I can't bear to look at him, unsure if I'll find pity or rage in his eyes. I need neither sentiment from him. From anyone.

He angles closer until I can't help but feel the heat of his gaze boring into the side of my face.

I know I don't have to answer him. My past is none of his business. But the way he grips the top of the fence as if he might snap it in two makes me think he might not take my silence for an answer.

"My first love," I finally admit. "Prince Cobalt."

"What did he do?" His voice is flat but edged with deadly calm.

"He manipulated me," I say as emotionlessly as I can. "Tricked me into giving him the power of my true name. He used fae magic to compel me to do terrible things. To hurt people. To...more than hurt them. And he hurt me too, simply by stripping me of control. But fret not," I say, my lips curling into a mirthless grin, "he's dead now. I watched the life fade from his eyes while I held his dying corpse."

A shudder crawls down my spine as I realize I uttered the last part out loud.

I'm about to cast a worried glance around, seeking anyone who might have overheard my violent confession, when something warm lands on my shoulder. Dante releases a slow and tremulous sigh, and gently turns me to face him. I tilt my chin, intending to give him a look of defiance, but my expression goes blank as I meet the intensity in his eyes. My breath catches at his proximity, at the spare inches that separate the fronts of our bodies, at the steady warmth of his palm on my shoulder.

"Albert would *never* hurt you," he says, each word punctuated. "Nor will I."

A flash of light sparks in my periphery. The photographer! How could I forget? He's too far to hear us from where he stands, but he can certainly see us. As can everyone in the queen's tent. My pulse kicks up, a thundering beat upon my already racing heart. Thank the All of All Dante and I probably look like a besotted couple, too entranced in each other's eyes to pay mind to the races, rather than two charlatans discussing my refusal to fall in love with my husband.

For appearances' sake, I force an adoring smile and place a hand on his chest. If my heart wasn't already raging, it would be now. Especially with the feel of his echoing beat hammering beneath my palm. "You, Your Highness, have a way of bringing up bleak subjects. Why should we speak of past pains and heartache when we could be discussing how dashing you look in that suit?"

He blinks at me a few times. After a dazed moment, his smile mirrors my own. He takes my hand from his chest and lifts the back of it to his lips. Closing his eyes, he presses his mouth to my silk glove. There he holds it in place, long enough to attract yet another flash of the camera. "My dearest Amelie, you are so right. I'm in a mood, aren't I?"

"You are." I tilt my head at the track. "Let us pay attention to the races."

Despite my outer composure, my heart continues to riot. It might be my imagination, but I feel as if the air around me and Dante has grown taut, buzzing with a strange energy. It has my every muscle coiled, aware of exactly how close Dante stands to me, attuned to his every breath, every shift in his stance. I can hardly pay attention to the derby. My eyes witness the competitors—kelpies, satyrs, fawns, and now centaurs—but my mind is elsewhere. Where it currently resides, I know not, for I don't want to investigate. It feels like it's wandering into dangerous territories I might not make it back from.

"Is it true centaurs have two penises?" Dante's jovial voice startles me. His light mood and crooked grin are so disarming, it makes me wonder if I imagined the thick tension I sensed.

Mirth bubbles in my chest as his ridiculous question echoes in my ears. Finally, a bark of laughter escapes my lips, far too loud than I intend. I cover my mouth with my hand, but not before a stuffy-looking matron in a dour gray gown gives me a disapproving look.

Trying my best to keep a giggle from overriding my words, I ask, "Why would you ask that?"

He shrugs, but the set of his shoulders reveals the pride he must feel at having amused me. "I heard a rumor. Besides, it wouldn't surprise me. Half man, half horse. Horse penis. Man penis. No?"

I have to cover my mouth again to smother my merriment. "No, Your Majesty, they do not have two penises."

He rubs his jaw, as if deep in serious thought, but his dimples give his levity away. His gaze follows the centaurs currently on the track. "Ah, you're right. I see only one, and I daresay they don't require more in that department.

However, is this their seelie or unseelie form? Can they fully shift between man and horse but simply choose to remain somewhere in the middle?"

I tilt my head, realizing I don't know the answer. Even after over twenty years living amongst the fae, many mysteries remain to me.

He continues. "And if they can shift between the two forms, wouldn't I be right, then? They technically *would* have two kinds of penises."

Another bark of laughter emerges from my lips, despite the hand still clamped over my mouth.

The old harpy of a woman gives me another glower, and I force myself to sober. I turn a far more subdued expression to Dante. "Perhaps you should ask one of the centaurs after the race. They are rumored to be rather virile creatures. I'm sure they'd be glad to talk about their...lower bits."

He leans closer to the fence and props an elbow upon it. The winner crosses the finish line, but Dante keeps his eyes on me. "That laugh is a lovely sound."

The strange tension between us snaps back into place. Then again...maybe I'm the only one who feels it.

He maintains his dashing devil-may-care grin, but his tone takes on a serious note. "You're so bold and bright, Amelie. Don't let society dim your light, no matter how much you want to earn their respect for your career. You shine bright enough with or without their approval. You're like a dazzling gemstone amongst unpolished rocks."

I swallow hard and pretend to take a keen interest in the fae stags that gather at the starting line for the next race. Playing off his compliment with a scoff, I mutter, "More like a blazing fire burning everything in her wake."

He leans close, bringing his face beneath the brim of my hat. I seize up, certain he's coming in for a kiss. Is there another photographer watching? But he doesn't bring his lips to mine, nor to my cheek. Instead, he brings his mouth by my ear, his breath caressing its shell. As he speaks, his deep voice rumbles through my very bones. "Were I not a spy but a man you met by happenstance, I would give anything to be burned by you."

Heat floods my heart, my chest, my cheeks, pooling like a molten lake low in my belly. I give him a playful shove, and he chuckles as he returns to his previous position at the fence. Meanwhile, I'm left reeling over a sudden realization that—in the split second where I pushed him away—I had a sudden urge to pull him closer instead.

But why? Because of a seductive compliment?

He's acting, I tell myself. Nothing he says or does is real. Everything is meant to get a rise out of me. To evoke a visual response appropriate for someone in love with her fiancé, all for the sake of our nearby witnesses.

The reminder manages to steady my heart. What it doesn't do is explain why the rise he got out of me felt so real.

15

The next two days bring only good news via paper. My meeting with the queen makes it into several respected periodicals, and all describe our interaction favorably, including her request for me to design her a dress. Even the scandal sheets treat me well, reporting on my obvious infatuation with my fiancé. These tidbits are accompanied by photographic evidence, either of Dante kissing my hand or whispering in my ear. Neither spark anything less than a tumultuous flutter in my chest when I look at them. I suppose that goes to show just how convincing we were. That's what I tell myself, at least.

Only one gossip column brought up my prior scandal, but it was only to say no one could doubt the prince and I are anything but a love match, and that anyone would be foolish to think our marriage was contrived just to counteract the unfortunate events at Bartleby's showcase.

I've even secured two new human clients, eager to

work with the designer who impressed Queen Ilma. It seems things can only get better, and that my next date with Dante—a gallery exhibit in the Spring Court—will surely gain me an even stronger footing with those I must impress.

But the third day following the derby delivers words on paper that have my heart sinking like a stone.

Dearest Amelie,

I regret to write this with all my heart, but I will not be able to attend tonight's date. An urgent matter has occurred, one I cannot in good conscience ignore. I wish I could simply turn my back on this matter and stand at your side tonight, but this, unfortunately, must take priority. Due to the location I must travel to, and the issue I must attend, I will have to meet you at the Galaxy Theater for our next date. Please forgive me. I promise you I would rather be with you than where I must be now.

Forever yours,
Albert

Despite the letter being signed by Albert—for appearances' sake, should I have received it in the presence of company—I know it was penned by Dante. I can almost hear his voice in every word. Regardless of the care taken to hide our ruse, I'm grateful I'm home alone and not at my studio, for if anyone else were to witness the wide grin that stretched my lips upon discovering a correspondence from my false prince only dip into a frown when I read the letter's contents, I'd have to explain the cause. And I'm not even sure I can explain it to myself. I shouldn't have felt so giddy at receiving a missive from Dante, nor should my lungs feel so tight like they do now. Anger would make more sense, as we had an agreement. Dante promised to attend my tour. Promised to make it to every event. But no matter how much I try to summon my rage, I feel only crushing disappointment.

I read the letter again, pacing my cottage from the living room to the kitchen and back again, nibbling my thumbnail all the while. The gown I was in the middle of altering when the post arrived stands ignored on its dress form. I was going to wear it tonight, as the dusty rose brocade garment has reached a level of near perfection with the addition of the rare dragon silk lace Foxglove gave me, but now I'm not sure I have the will to complete my task. I can't go to the gallery alone. Not when Dante and I have made so much progress in the public eye as a couple. Arriving alone will only arouse negative speculation. How dare he put me in such a position! What could be so important that he'd cancel our date?

My next thought is a ludicrous one, but I think it nonetheless.

He's pulling away. We got too close at the derby, too honest about our pasts, and now he's retreating.

I shake the thought from my head, reminding myself our relationship is fake. There's nothing to pull away from. Even if we were a real couple, obsessing over whether a man is in emotional retreat from me is something a younger Amelie would have done. Not the woman I am now. A woman who cares not for love.

I pace back toward the kitchen and read the letter once more, this time with a rational state of mind. I linger over certain parts, assessing what may be hidden between the lines.

An urgent matter has occurred.

...this, unfortunately, must take priority.

I recall the last time he spoke of priority. It was when we first met and I confronted him over his behavior at the Salty Satyr, before I knew he wasn't the real Albert. When I asked if he cared about forging peace between Faerwyvae and Bretton, he said it was his *utmost priority*. It makes sense now, knowing he's a spy and decoy, tasked with ensuring Albert truly is safe here and that our alliance isn't a façade. If the words in his letter are true, then the matter that keeps him from attending our date must have to do with his mission. Perhaps he was attacked like he was in the alleyway after our dinner. Perhaps he's gathered leads on why members of the Durrely Boys targeted us in the first place. The prince—or worse, Dante—could be in true danger.

Shame heats my cheeks, mingling with anxiety over Dante's well-being. How could I be so selfish? Of course he'd only cancel our date for good reason.

The chastisement does little to alleviate my unexpected disappointment, but it does fuel me with a sudden urge to finish my gown. With renewed vigor, I return to the dress form and assess my creation. I may not be able to wear my gown to tonight's canceled date, but I can wear it to our next rendezvous. And now that I'm looking at it, I'm starting to think of a few new improvements I can make to the design, ones that will have Dante regretting that he almost missed me wearing it.

Taking up my needle and thread, I shove my lingering worry over Dante's safety to the back of my mind and proceed to finish what I intend to be my most stunning creation yet.

Two days later, I'm in a hansom cab in the city of Lumenas—Star Court's most popular destination for entertainment—heading for the Galaxy Theater. The evening streets sparkle with spotlights and glowing marquees, the sidewalks crowded with tourists and street performers. I notice most of the former are human while the latter are more commonly fae. But as much as I try to focus on the dazzling sights the city offers, my mind continues to drift.

I fidget with one of the lace rosettes embellishing my skirt in an attempt to channel the frenetic energy coursing through me. The only correspondence I've received from Dante since he canceled our last date was a short letter that assured me he'd meet me inside the theater's atrium. Still, part of me worries he won't show.

My cab slows as it rounds the corner of the next street, one far less boisterous than the last. Here, street performers and awed tourists give way to subdued aristocrats in evening finery. This part of town caters to the upper class. Instead of raucous music halls, clubs, and daring fae performances, this street hosts opera houses and elegant theaters. My cab pulls to a stop behind a long row of other coaches. Up ahead I see a brightly lit marquee that reads *Across the Glittering Plains Starring Holly Abercrombie*. On each side of the marquee stand brass stanchions draped with velvet ropes to segment the dozens upon dozens of reporters and photographers from the guests who exit their coaches to attend the play.

Across the Glittering Plains is said to be an epic tale of romance and betrayal, and is insanely popular in Bretton. It's making its debut in Faerwyvae tonight at this very theater and even stars the same leading actress that brought the play to fame in Bretton. Needless to say, this is a major event, and with the play's popularity amongst humans, it will be brimming with my ideal clientele. More importantly, it's been deemed worthy of a red-carpet premiere, replete with a walk down the aisle for the most elite guests in attendance, and will be captured by press from all over Faerwyvae.

I just so happen to have snagged a place for myself and my fiancé on that coveted red carpet—a golden opportunity to show off my work in a way that will garner attention far and wide. But if Dante isn't here...

Panic crawls up my throat, but I do my best to swallow it down. He said he'd meet me in the atrium, which means he's already inside. Or will be soon. Either way, I can do this without him. Some may speculate on why we've arrived separately, but I'm hoping my gown—and the other famous guests—will overshadow any such rumors that may arise.

I angle myself closer to my cab window and watch as a couple emerges from the coach parked before the theater entrance. Nausea turns in my stomach as I recognize the familiar profile of Maureen Vance. Of course she had to be here tonight. At least enough coaches stand between hers and mine that I don't have to worry about encountering her or her lecherous husband. Red carpet walks are slow processions. Tonight's walk will start with each guest's exit from their vehicle, followed by a stroll down the stairs from the lobby to the atrium, then ending with a round of questions from reporters before we move on to find our seats in the auditorium.

I narrow my eyes as Mrs. Vance starts off down the red carpet, pausing to wave as flash bulbs go off. She's the same age as Mr. Vance—about ten years older than I am —but carries herself with a far more regal bearing than her libertine husband. I hate to admit she looks fetching in her black satin gown and mink stole. Her gray-brown hair has been curled and pinned in a low twist, showing off enormous pearl earrings. I see no sign of Mr. Vance, so at least I'm not the only attached woman who arrived alone. Besides, it's expected for couples to walk separately down the aisle during the grand entrance, as it's meant to display one's ensemble in full detail. The interviews in the atrium, however, are often held with couples— should they attend with an escort—and I'd rather not address any questions regarding my lack of fiancé.

Which means Dante damn well better be inside.

With each coach that pulls away from the entrance, shortening the time until it's my turn, it grows harder to steady my breathing. This won't be my first time walking a red carpet, but my previous experiences were for fae events, which are often more whimsical and chaotic than what I see presented beneath the theater's marquee now. And this is certainly the first that feels like it carries such high stakes. My reputation. My career. My future.

The coach-and-four in front of my cab pulls up to the red carpet, deposits its well-dressed cargo, and exits the queue far faster than I'm ready for. My hansom takes its predecessor's place, making my heart slam against my ribs. I almost expect a steady hand to fall on my shoulder or a whispered voice telling me I'll do fine, but then I remember Dante isn't here to settle me with his cool confidence.

It's just me.

Alone.

For decades, I've liked being alone. And while I still value my independence and personal renown, something has changed. There's a hollow pit inside my chest, growing wider by the day. A pit that once was filled with rage and hatred, then was masked with apathy before I sealed it off and buried it to die with my past. The pit has somehow been revived and is now eager for the sustenance that brought it back to life.

But what is that sustenance? What nourishment do I crave? I don't dare try to answer.

Closing my eyes, I steel myself against such soft and aimless musings.

The previous guests have now entered the theater doors, which means it's my turn to make my grand entrance. A human usher dressed in a red and black suit steps toward my cab and opens my door. With a steadying breath, I gracefully slide from my seat and take his hand. As soon as my heeled shoes meet the plush red velvet lining the ground before me, flash bulbs begin to pop. Keeping my steps slow and swaying, I saunter down the aisle, pausing to pose every few feet, angling my body this way and that to give the photographers several angles to admire my dress. My bustled train trails behind me while every inch of the dragon silk lace that adorns my bodice and skirt ripples with fluttering movement, as delicate as the wings of a butterfly. A gasp comes from a nearby reporter, followed by awed mutterings containing the words *stunning, gorgeous*, and *phenomenal*.

A bright feeling loosens inside me, and my confidence flares with it. My next steps down the carpet feel easier, my hips swaying, my chest lifting. The latter helps draw attention to the latest addition I made—a lower neckline, plus a keyhole cutout in the fabric at the center of my bust, revealing a glimpse at the inner curves of my breasts. It's a bit daring for a dress meant to attract human favor, considering their propensity for more modest designs, but as another reporter exclaims *sexy* and *provocative* in the most admiring of tones, I think I added just enough sensual allure after all.

By the time I reach the theater doors, I'm exhilarated, burning with a sense of pride and confidence I haven't felt since I was younger. The ushers inside the lobby direct me toward the stairs that lead down to the theater's atrium. More photographers line the steps, catching shots of the woman currently walking down them. At the base of the stairs, dozens of patrons gather, loitering about in the most graceful of ways—chatting, making introductions, or merely standing around looking fashionable. Beyond them, the queue for the interview begins.

The woman in front of me reaches the bottom of the steps and heads for the back of the queue. I'm about to take my first step down the crimson carpeted stairs when something catches my eye. Something—or *someone*, I should say—I was too distracted to notice before.

But I notice now, for there at the bottom of the steps, staring up at me with a dimpled smile, is Dante.

16

For a moment, Dante seems entranced. Or perhaps I'm the one who's captivated. I don't think I've ever seen the spy looking so dashing, so incredibly handsome, as he does now. His black suit fits his body like a glove, showing off his tall, lean frame, the wide cut of his shoulders. His golden hair is swept back from his face, drawing attention to his glittering blue eyes and sharp jawline. Like always, he carries his cane, but his poise makes it seem more like a scepter. If I didn't know Dante was a spy or that his cane doubled as a lethal weapon, I would think he was the most regal man alive.

Has he always been this beautiful? Or am I simply wrapped up in the elegance around me?

An usher gestures to remind me it's my turn to descend the stairs. I give him a gracious nod, then slowly make my way past the photographers, stopping to pose and smile for the cameras. Halfway down the steps, I catch Dante's eyes again. I'm so caught off guard by his expression that I nearly lose my footing. His mouth hangs on its hinge as his gaze sweeps over every inch of me. When our eyes lock, his still-parted lips curl into an even wider smile, and he brings a hand to his heart as if he's been overcome with emotion.

I know it's probably an act—no, it *is* an act—but I can't help relishing his response just the same. In this moment, I feel like the most beautiful woman in the world. Warmth courses through me, so pleasant and euphoric, I feel like I'm glowing with it. I hold Dante's gaze as I take the remaining steps, basking in the heat of his admiring stare.

As soon as my feet touch the floor, he makes a beeline for me. My heart races as we meet each other in a familiar yet formal embrace—his hand at my lower back, my palms propped on his shoulders—the way a madly-in-love engaged couple would be expected to meet. We didn't plan to embrace like this for the public eye, but it feels natural. Better than natural. Based on the flash bulbs that shine our way, the press is enjoying it as much as I am.

Dante's mouth brushes my cheek in a chaste kiss before I have the good sense to comprehend it's the first time his lips have touched anything but the back of my gloved hand. Just when I expect him to pull away, I feel him linger.

"Gods, you look amazing." The slight growl infused in his tone has heat burning low in my belly.

He releases me, leaving me flustered at the sudden space between us. Then I feel the warmth of his hand lingering at my lower back, a touch that is both steadying and exciting at once.

"You don't look so bad yourself," I say, finding my voice amidst my stupor.

He gestures his cane toward the interview queue but keeps his eyes on me. "Shall we? Or would you like to linger?" When I don't immediately answer, his lips quirk up at one corner. "There are certainly parts of you I wouldn't mind lingering over."

His seductive teasing manages to cut the rest of the way through the daze I find myself in. My mind clears, and I let out a playful laugh. "You're too brash, Your Highness."

"And you are too damn stunning not to be."

My cheeks warm with a traitorous blush. Hopefully my layers of rouge and cosmetics are able to hide it.

Dante—much to my ludicrous disappointment— removes his hand from my lower back and offers me his arm instead. I take it, and with all proper refinement, we make our way to the back of the queue.

THE FIRST SEVERAL INTERVIEWS ARE BRIEF, WITH THE reporters asking me and Dante some variation of the same questions: if we're excited to see the play, if we can share any details regarding our upcoming wedding, and who we're wearing tonight. I try to evade the topic of our nuptials, as I have nothing exciting to share on that front. Per my request, my wedding to the prince will be a sober affair—nothing more than signing our names on a contract. Questions about my ensemble, on the other hand, I address with no small amount of enthusiasm. Dante too speaks about his attire with pride. I'm unsurprised to discover his suit was made by a famous designer from Bretton who works exclusively for the royal family. The cut is slightly different from the styles popular in Faerwyvae, and the fabrics are certainly of royal quality. I imagine serving as the prince's decoy comes with the benefit of having a royal wardrobe tailored with precision.

We continue down the red carpet, pausing for more photographs and interview questions. Everything is going perfectly. Better than I imagined. That is, until we near the end of the row of reporters, and I spot the last person I care to come into close contact with tonight— Mrs. Vance. How is she still on the red carpet? She arrived well before me. She stands chatting with a reporter, back facing me and Dante. I freeze in place, torn between accepting more interviews and exiting the red carpet at once.

"What is it?" Dante asks, following my line of sight. "Ah. It's her."

Despite having met only Howard Vance at the restaurant, he seems to have no trouble identifying the source of my distress. He steers me toward a reporter on the opposite side of the carpet. My relief is short-lived, for that's when I recognize a tall, lanky man with dark, slicked-back hair. He's the reporter Lydia Mangrove brought to barge in on me in the fitting room with Mr. Vance.

A slight arch of his brow is the only sign of recognition he shows. I'm about to ask Dante to shift course again, but before I can say a word, the reporter steals my companion's attention.

"Prince Albert, I'm Eaton Farris. Who are you wearing tonight?"

I do my best to keep my composure as Dante guides us toward him. As the spy answers the other man's question, I cast a glowing smile to our neighboring reporters, hoping to catch their eyes. Unfortunately, those nearby are actively engaged in interviews, and none seem eager for an excuse to extricate themselves from the conversation. Unlike me. Though, perhaps if I keep my focus anywhere but Eaton Farris, he'll take the hint and not speak a word to me.

Commotion at the middle of the queue provides a genuine distraction. I angle my head this way and that, trying to see what has the flash bulbs popping several times faster than before while reporters and their interviewees halt mid-conversation.

"It's Holly Abercrombie!" someone exclaims from nearby. That's when I see a tall, slim human female with long blonde hair worn loose around her shoulders. She wears an old-fashioned dress and apron, which tells me she must be in costume. I'm surprised the starlet isn't backstage, what with the play starting so soon. She waves for the cameras, pausing to chat with only a select few reporters or guests.

I reluctantly divert my attention from the actress to my partner, hoping Dante has finished speaking to Mr. Farris, only to find his attention is fixed on Holly Abercrombie. His jaw is tight, eyes slightly narrowed. Mr. Farris stares expectantly at the spy as if he's awaiting an answer to a question Dante left hanging. But Dante doesn't seem at all aware of the reporter anymore, his interest fully taken by the actress.

He isn't the only one, I tell myself, but it doesn't stop my chest from feeling tight.

Mr. Farris leans forward to find the source of his interviewee's engrossment. When he does, a smirk twists his ratlike face. "Prince Albert," the reporter says, voice louder this time.

Dante blinks rapidly and swivels back toward Mr. Farris. "Yes, sorry," he says with a sheepish grin. "What was the question?"

The way Mr. Farris lifts his chin and narrows his eyes has my stomach sinking. It's the same expression I saw on his face when he found me and Mr. Vance in the fitting room. I squeeze Dante's arm, hoping I can convey the warning I feel brewing in my gut.

But it's too late.

"Is it true you and Holly Abercrombie arrived at the theater together tonight?"

The blood leaves my face, and Dante stiffens at my side.

"Excuse me?" The words leave my mouth, conveying the full weight of my shock before I gain control over my countenance.

"Our interview is done," Dante says and takes a step away.

"And is it true the two of you dined together three days ago and spent the night at a hotel together the evening before last?"

Dante takes another step away, but my feet anchor in place, separating us.

The questions slice through me like an iron blade. Dante was seen with the actress...three days ago? That was the day before he missed our date at the gallery.

And the night before last was when I got his letter canceling our plans for some important matter that took priority.

This...*she*...was his important matter?

Rage burns my blood, heating it to a boiling point until I feel flames lace my palms. It takes all my restraint to keep my fire at bay, to force my flames to recede before they can char my gloves.

Dante, finding me no longer holding his arm, returns to me. Standing between me and Mr. Farris to block the reporter from view, he whispers low, "Amelie, ignore him—"

"Ah, Miss Abercrombie! Over here!"

I freeze at the sound of the name on Mr. Farris' lips, but even more so at the feminine voice that answers, "Oh, hello!"

Wasting no time, Mr. Farris asks, "Miss Abercrombie, were you aware that Prince Albert was engaged to Miss Fairfield when you dined with him the evening of the twenty-second?"

My heart rages as a flush of heat crawls up my neck. This time, it's more than just anger that has me so discomposed. Now that the actress has approached Mr. Farris, all eyes are on us.

Holly Abercrombie pulls up short, her head swinging to the side where she finds Dante. Her eyes go wide at finding him there, but she doesn't bother sparing a glance at me. I don't miss the subtle nod he gives her.

In a flash, a coy smile takes over Miss Abercrombie's perfect face. She flutters her lashes at the reporter, then gives Dante's shoulder an affectionate pat. "He and I have been acquainted for many, many years. We are good friends. Any encounters we've had since I arrived in Faer-wyvae have been strictly platonic."

Her words do nothing to cool my inner fire. She didn't deny having dined with him. Instead, she basically admitted Mr. Farris' intel is accurate.

"Sources say the two of you were caught acting more than platonic," Mr. Farris says.

She gives a flippant wave of her hand. "Sources, as you say, love to exaggerate. Thank you so much for the interview, but I really must be heading backstage." With a placid smile, she gracefully exits the interview and brushes by, pausing only to offer Dante a curtsy and me a respectful nod.

Meanwhile, I can manage nothing more than a clenching of my teeth. Dante places his hand at my lower back, but I flinch away from his touch. My lungs grow tighter by the second while my head spins, reeling in the wake of Dante's dishonesty, the reporter's callous questions, the attention of those nearby still fixated on us. And—strangely—perhaps a pinch of fiery hot jealousy.

Dante takes my hand in his, weaving our fingers tightly together as he guides me away from Mr. Farris. As much as I want to wrench my hand away, I know we need to keep up appearances. Or do we? Was everything I've been working for just smashed to smithereens? I'm too flustered to think clearly, to analyze how much damage was just done to my reputation. To my upcoming marriage and the façade of love we were supposed to maintain.

It's *his* fault. Dante did this. He ruined everything.

A sob builds in my chest, and I stumble over my shoes.

Dante pauses to help me right myself. "Amelie..." My whispered name carries some strangled emotion I can't identify.

Just as I manage to lift my chin and take a steady step, Mr. Farris' too-loud voice calls out from behind me. "Miss Fairfield, how do you feel knowing your fiancé is on such familiar terms with a beautiful actress?"

Dante squeezes my fingers. "Pay him no heed," he mutters through his teeth. "I'll explain—"

"Does it not bother you because of your own recent scandal? Are you aware that the Vances are getting a divorce? Do you think you might be the cause? Do you consider yourself a homewrecker?"

Before I realize what's happening, Dante releases my hand and bolts behind me. I whirl to find him standing before Mr. Farris, one hand clamped around the man's cravat, the other holding the length of his cane against the reporter's throat. Dante's voice comes out low and deadly. "Watch your mouth when speaking about my fiancé if you value your tongue. Otherwise, I'll cut it out of your throat."

Silence echoes in the wake of Dante's threat. Sweat beads at my brow as I realize it isn't just those nearby who are staring. *Everyone* is looking at us. Including—much to my horror—Mrs. Vance. Her lips are curled in a wicked grin, revealing just how much she's relishing the spectacle.

I rush over to Dante and tug the sleeve of his jacket. "Albert," I hiss, infusing my tone with the reminder of who he's supposed to be right now—a cowardly, roguish prince, not a violent spy.

Dante's shoulders tremble as he maintains hold on

the reporter. Mr. Farris' face has gone as white as a sheet. I utter the prince's name again, which finally gets through to him. With a long, heavy sigh, he releases the man and dons a toothy smile that is far more menacing than kind. With more force than necessary, he straightens Mr. Farris' cravat, eyes locked on his. "Are we clear?"

The reporter's throat bobs before he dips his chin in an unsteady nod.

Dante returns to me, but I can't look him in the eye. Emotions war within me—anger, envy, embarrassment, gratitude. The latter is the most out of place. I shouldn't feel grateful Dante threatened a man on my behalf. Not after what he did. Not after he lied to me so he could be with someone else.

Flames lick my palms again, and this time, I don't think I can smother them. Already, I feel my silk gloves beginning to singe. Without a second thought, I lift the hem of my skirt and flee.

17

It occurs to me, as I flee the red carpet, that I'm going the wrong way. If I wanted out of the theater, I should have left in the opposite direction from where I'm going now. But that would have forced me past all those judging eyes, all those rows and rows of photographers and reporters. I would have had to make a shameful walk back up the staircase, spoiling my elegant entrance. Not that my graceful first impression matters now. Everything is ruined.

Ruined.

I dart into the auditorium, where the seats have begun to fill with those who've finished their interviews. A few faces turn my way, alerted by my frantic pace. I know I should slow down, settle my composure, and try to make less of a scene, but with rage still searing my blood—and heating my palms with tiny flames—my foremost priority is to get somewhere private first. If I don't, fire will erupt from my every pore, and everyone will see it.

See *me*.

The real me.

The deadly me.

Sweat slicks my palms as I skirt around the back of the auditorium and exit out a side door. Thankfully, the promise of sanctuary beckons on the other side in the form of the women's powder room. I charge straight for it, curling my fingers into fists in an attempt to smother my flames. But as soon as the powder room door closes behind me, red fire envelops my hands, burning away my gloves. I stifle a yelp as I frantically beat my hands against my dress, realizing my folly too late. A line of lace ignites at once. My shock manages to calm my anger from a roar to a simmer, allowing me to get control of the fire surging from my palms.

With a far more level head, I race to the sink and douse my hands in water. The effect is immediate, extinguishing my flames and sending steam rising into the air. Now for my skirt...

"Oh my!" A woman emerges from one of the toilet stalls, pulling up short when she sees me. A second follows from the stall beside her. Both stare at me and my burning dress with horror.

"Your skirt," says the second woman. "It...it's on fire!"

With my now-wet hands, I beat the line of burning lace. "It's nothing," I say in a rush, forcing a smile to my lips. As I continue to try and smother my flames, grinning as if I'm simply dealing with an inconvenient stain, I realize I don't come across as reassuring at all. I seem positively manic.

The two women exchange a glance, then frown down

at my efforts with distaste. One opens her mouth to speak but can't seem to find her words.

"I'm fine," I say. "Totally fine."

That's all the permission they need to bolt from the powder room with haste. My disquiet cools tenfold now that I no longer have an audience. Even more so when I note my burning lace isn't spreading to any other part of my dress. In fact, burning isn't quite the word for what's happening to the lace.

My brows knit together as I bend forward and take a closer look. The flames are contained to the lace, and they don't consume it like my red fire did to my gloves. Instead, the blaze is a pale shade of gold that dances over the lace in gentle, flickering waves. The heat the fire generates isn't searing either. Instead, it's a soft warmth.

I brush my hand over the lace, and the flames disappear, leaving not a hint of charred fabric to be seen.

"What in the world..." I mutter under my breath, puzzling over such a strange phenomenon. "Why wouldn't it burn?"

The answer comes to me at once: dragon silk lace.

Foxglove said silk dragons weave their nests from the silk and utilize it to keep their hatchlings warm. He also said their habitat is in the northern forests of the Spring Court. It stands to reason that the dragon silk evolved to withstand high temperatures and keep a flame burning for long periods of time. Not only that, but to do so without catching on the surrounding flora and fauna.

I'm so fascinated, I almost forget where I am. What I ran from.

Then the powder room door swings open, and all my prior emotions return.

Dante pauses in the doorway, eyes sweeping over me and landing on the tattered remnants of my gloves—nothing more than a band of charred silk circling my upper arms. Then his gaze moves to my skirt, and his eyes go wide. He starts forward, my name flying from his lips, pitched with panic.

I glance down at my skirt, noticing a piece of flaming lace I hadn't extinguished. Before Dante can reach me, I sweep my hand over the golden fire, dusting it away.

Then I turn a glare on him. "What are you doing in here?"

He halts at my sharp tone, his body going tense. One hand opens and closes at his side while the other grips the head of his cane. When he speaks, his voice is controlled. Strained. "You shouldn't have run, Amelie. We could have salvaged—"

"Don't you dare tell me what I shouldn't have done!"

"I promise you, I'm going to fix this."

"Fix this?" I bark a humorless laugh. "You've *ruined* this. You made a fool of me with that...that actress. Worse, you lied about it. You lied to me, claiming you had some important mission that made you cancel our date. I hate that I believed you. That I was so foolish as to worry—"

I swallow my words before I can admit I was ever concerned over his safety or well-being.

The sound of the door opening again has my pulse hammering. If Dante followed me, a reporter could have too. But no, the woman in the doorway is but a guest. She halts, face paling as she sees Dante standing before me.

Keeping his eyes locked on mine, Dante extends his arm and points his cane at the interloper. "Out."

The woman scurries out faster than she came.

Once the door closes, he steps closer. "It's not what you think."

"Holly Abercrombie admitted to having dined with you. I saw how you reacted when Eaton Farris asked if the two of you arrived at the theater together. How could you be so careless?" My hand flies involuntarily to my chest, demonstrating the words I won't say. *How could you be so careless...with my heart?*

"It wasn't me she dined with. It was Albert."

I scoff. "You expect me to believe that? She said '*he and I* have been acquainted for many years,' not '*the prince* and I.' And she touched your shoulder when she said it. If she truly has known you—or the prince—for long, then she knows better than to get the two of you confused. Isn't that what you said? Those close to the prince would never mistake him for his decoy?"

He runs his hand through his hair, sending his well-styled tresses into disarray. "Did you expect her to blow my cover? To admit to the reporter that the man posing as Albert was a fraud?"

"You're avoiding giving a direct answer," I say, although I admit I feel a bit abashed at his explanation. He's right. If anyone was friendly with Dante or Albert, they would know to act accordingly without outing Dante's mission. Still, it doesn't cool my anger.

Finally, he says, "Yes, Holly and I were acquainted."

A shard of ice pierces my heart. "Romantically?"

He opens his mouth, but before he can answer, I wave my hand at him.

"No, it doesn't matter," I say, my words tasting of lies. "You can be romantically involved with anyone you want, and the same goes for Albert. All I asked for was discretion, and you failed me."

"That's why..." His jaw tightens, and he begins to drum his fingers against the head of his cane. I'm familiar enough with the gesture to know it means he's fighting not to say something. He's probably trying to sort out how to best lie to me. "It's just...it's complicated."

I fold my arms and lift my chin. "It's not. An old flame came to town, and you couldn't help but reconnect with her—"

"No, that's not..." He steps closer, his gaze intense, pleading. "Hear me out, Amelie, please. Yes, I knew her. And, yes, for a time, I courted her. Long ago."

"I don't need to hear any of this." I throw my hands in the air and try to skirt around him, but he mirrors my every step.

"Then she got me to introduce her to Albert," he says in a rush. "And she chose *him*."

I pause midstep and glance up at his face. There's a wounded quality to his expression, and it makes my chest feel tight. But wounded or not, it doesn't prove he didn't abandon me to meet with *her*.

"They've been on and off for years," Dante says. "I had no idea she was coming to Faerwyvae, but Albert did. They've both known since before this marriage was first arranged. He knew about the play and planned on reconnecting with Holly during her stay on the isle. If I'd known he'd be—"

He shakes his head, averting his gaze, and slams the end of his cane onto the carpeted floor so hard, I'm surprised it doesn't pierce a hole into it.

Then, with a heavy sigh, he returns his attention to

me. His eyes turn down at the corners as his shoulders sink. Even his voice dips low, as if crushed by a leaden weight. "If I'd known he'd be so foolish as to compromise your reputation, I would have tied him to a chair, prince or no."

My breaths grow shallow beneath the earnestness in Dante's eyes.

"Albert snuck away from his guards and dined publicly with Holly in Port Dellaray. They were seen kissing, touching. I escorted her here to ensure neither she nor Albert did anything idiotic. She was half convinced to quit the show and stay with Albert at his hotel. I knew I couldn't let that happen, for it would only be a matter of time before the two of them snuck out in public again. Miss Abercrombie can't handle being out of the spotlight for long."

He says it matter-of-factly, with neither bitterness nor fondness. It helps ease the spike of jealousy that made its home in my heart.

His lips curl in disgust, and his tone darkens. "I promise you, Amelie, I had no idea Albert would do such a thing. I told him about your rules, told him that protecting your reputation was equally as important as forging peace between Faerwyvae and Bretton. I thought he understood. That he valued your marriage. Now I see that I confused my own ideals for his, assuming we were of one mind. But even our hearts were in different places."

The way he says *hearts* in that strained, anguished tone has my breath catching. My pulse flutters in a terrifying rhythm. One I'm not ready to hear yet.

I step away from him but manage to gain only a few

inches of space before my back comes up against the quartz counter of the sink behind me.

"I'm so sorry," Dante says. "I did everything I could to control the damage done. As soon as Albert's guards got word to me about what happened, I made haste to Port Dellaray. I reminded Albert what was at stake. Told him I would rather turn traitor and end his life than see him humiliate you. After that, I hunted down every reporter in the area, every photographer, and bribed, threatened, and stole the story from them. Yet it seems my efforts weren't thorough enough."

A surge of warmth runs through me. He went through all that trouble...for me? I shake the thought from my head, reminding myself that I have more reasons to be upset with him.

I purse my lips, standing tall to hide how badly I wish I could retreat from him. "I don't need you to save me."

He frowns, brows knitting together. "You would have rather I let Albert's indiscretions reach the papers?"

"No, that...that was acceptable. What you didn't need to do was attack a reporter on my behalf."

He has the decency to look ashamed, but when he opens his mouth, it isn't to apologize. "He's lucky I didn't slit his throat on the spot."

My eyes go wide. "Excuse me?"

He steels his expression. "His words were unforgiveable. His demeanor was detestable. To call you a...a homewrecker—"

I gesture at him. "This is what I mean. I don't need you doing *this* for me. I don't need *anyone* saving me. Ever."

"You may not need saving, but you are worthy of it nonetheless. You deserve to be defended by your fiancé."

"You're not my fiancé."

He takes in a sharp breath. His countenance flickers with the barest hint of sorrow. "Trust me. I know."

My throat feels tight, and part of me wants to apologize. For what, I'm not sure. All I know is that my anger is in danger of slipping away. If it does, I don't know what it will leave behind. Something too soft and vulnerable, probably. Gathering the cooling embers of my rage, I do my best to rekindle them. I narrow my eyes to a glare. "What's that supposed to mean?"

He steps closer and places his cane on the counter behind me. I gasp, leaning back as far as I can as he props his palms on the edge of the counter, framing my waist with his hands. My breaths grow sharper, faster.

With burning intensity, he holds my gaze. "You know what it means."

I shake my head, unable to disentangle words from my tongue.

His eyes search mine, and he leans closer, stopping only when our faces are mere inches apart. His voice turns to a whisper. "Tell me you don't feel it too."

"Feel what?" I say, far breathier than I intend.

His throat bobs. "Feel...the spark between us."

As if in answer, heat surges from my heart, spreading over my body in a tingling warmth. Despite how pleasant it feels, it's a dangerous sensation, one I haven't felt in decades.

The last time I felt this way...

No. No, I can't let myself feel like that again.

Training my expression into a cold mask, I say, "How could I have feelings for you? We're fake."

A ghost of a smirk plays over his lips. "Are we?"

"Yes."

"Maybe for you. For me...well, very little of what I've said or done around you has been fake."

"You're just acting. You're playing a part."

He leans ever closer, and a traitorous thrill buzzes low in my belly. Slowly, he takes one hand off the counter and closes over my bare palm. With the tenderest care, he brings my hand to his chest, slipping it beneath his jacket, then his waistcoat, until only the smooth fabric of his shirt stands between my palm and the pounding drum. "Does this feel fake?"

My mind spins, dizzy as it dances to the tune his heart plays for me.

He runs his thumb over the back of my hand. "You've consumed me, Amelie Fairfield. I've thought of little else but you since we met at the Salty Satyr."

"Why?" The word comes out part sigh, part question.

"What do you mean *why*?" His dimples deepen as his lips stretch into a wide smile. "Because you're...incredible. Beautiful, yes, but brilliant too. You're creative. Talented. Funny. And when you show me that flirtatious side—just a hint of lust—it drives me wild."

The word *lust* sends a ripple of fear through me. Lust was once my demise. But somehow, when he says it, it feels like it might be the greatest virtue.

He speaks again. "The only acting I've done is pretending you don't completely disarm me."

The buzzing warmth increases inside me, filling every inch of my mind, body, and soul, and sending every trace of fear scattering. His heart continues to slam into my palm, and the pleasure it brings is more euphoric than the most intoxicating fae wine.

His expression falters, turning more serious. "If you don't feel it too..."

Before I can think better of it, I gather up his other hand and bring it to my chest. My eyelids flutter closed at the feel of his palm against the upper curve of my breast. It heaves against his hand, and I wonder if he can even feel the beat of my heart through the rapid pulse of my lungs. When I dare to open my eyes, Dante's face hovers over mine, lips parted, gaze rich with want.

I haven't seen that look in so long, but I recognize it. It draws out the fiery part of me I've tried so hard to smother down.

With a sly grin, I free my hand from under his, sliding it from his chest to behind his neck. Then, tilting my head back, I drink in the increasing desire flooding his blue irises. It fuels my boldness like a heady nectar.

"Amelie," he says, half whisper, half groan, "tell me what you want."

"Kiss me," I say, my tone far more demanding than his.

Without hesitation, he obeys.

18

His lips crush into mine, and I melt into him, pulling him closer to me. A sense of pride mingles with the pleasant warmth still burning inside me. It grows as I feel him come undone in my arms, eliciting a deep groan against my mouth. I echo the sound with a soft sigh and part my lips to sweep my tongue against his. His hand stiffens against my upper breast, still closed over my heart, and my pride glows brighter. In this moment I have power over him, dominance, even as I yield and soften. It's something I haven't fully experienced since I was younger, back when lust was my second language. Back then, I experienced this feeling on the regular, sought it out. I didn't think I wanted to feel this way anymore. Not after the trouble this sort of behavior once got me in. But now, with him...

It's all I want.

I tilt my head, letting our kiss deepen. With one arm, he reaches behind me and hefts me onto the counter. Lifting my skirts slightly, I widen my legs so he can stand between them. We close even more space until none remains. I lace my hands through his hair and arch into his touch, drawing attention to the less-than-chaste positioning of his hand. He obliges my wordless request, trailing his fingers from the upper curve of my breast, down to the skin along the deep, lacy neckline of my dress, then to cup me fully. Thank the All of All I'm not wearing a corset with my gown—due to the keyhole cutout in the bust—and can feel the warmth of his palm. His lips leave mine to brush my cheek, the lobe of my ear, then down the column of my neck.

"Amelie." Dante groans my name against my collarbone, his grip tightening on my breast. I throw my head back, aching for more of his lips, his touch, his—

"Miss Fairfield!"

The unwelcome voice douses my desire. Dante stiffens, and we both swivel our heads toward the door. There Maureen Vance stands, hands on her hips as she casts her condemning gaze at us.

Dante takes a step back, releasing me to slide off the counter. But it's too late. She saw the position we were in, saw his hand groping my breast. Rage burns through me, a deep and monstrous thing that rails against having to treat something as beautiful as an impassioned kiss like something shameful. Even as I acknowledge my ire, I know the fault lies with me. Dante and I shared a heated kiss in a public powder room at a human social event. I should have known better. I *do* know better.

Lust, some bitter part of me taunts. *Romance. They will always be your ruin.*

Mrs. Vance stomps forward, mouth agape. She tries to look scandalized, but I can tell she's far more smug than shocked. Another woman follows behind her, and I wonder if she saw too. From her pale face and her too-wide eyes, I think she must have. In fact, she might be the woman who tried to enter the room when Dante first came in, before he ordered her out. I was too focused on Dante then, but damn it, of course she would have told someone. A man being caught alone with a woman in a powder room is cause enough for scandal. Whether she told someone to gain help in saving my virtue or to expose my misdeed, it matters not. The damage is done.

A public display of amorous affection is one of the worst social crimes in human society, regardless of whether the kiss is between strangers, engaged lovers, or a married couple. It simply isn't done.

"How vulgar!" Mrs. Vance shouts. "Have you no respect for this fine establishment? Clearly you have none for yourself."

Dante takes a forbidding step toward the woman, but I still him, placing my hand on his forearm. He halts at once and straightens his coat and cravat. Then, with deadly calm, he retrieves his cane from the counter. "Fret not," he says through his teeth. "My fiancée and I were just leaving. Miss Fairfield is feeling unwell and nearly fainted. I was attending to her, as you saw just now."

It's a terrible lie, one that couldn't possibly convince anyone who saw us with their own eyes. Others, though, may believe the story. Especially those who witnessed me rushing from the red carpet in such haste.

Dante takes my hand and leads us toward the door. That's when I see several other women crowding the hall. Did they too catch us kissing but were too polite to do anything but scurry away?

I try to keep my head held high as we pass Mrs. Vance, despite needing to play the part of the fainting maiden. For her, I will not debase myself.

She scoffs as we reach the doorway. "Holly Abercrombie must have been unwell too, Your Highness. Do you attend to all women the same way? Or just the loose ones?"

Dante pauses midstep, chest heaving. A vein pulses at his temple, and I'm certain he's on the verge of doing something reckless. I know because his rage is my own, burning my blood and threatening to explode from my palms like before.

Giving Dante's hand a reassuring squeeze, I look over my shoulder with a saccharine smile. "Maybe you should ask your husband instead. He's quite the expert at giving unwanted attention to women, is he not? Good evening, Maureen. I do hope you enjoy the play."

With that, Dante and I march from the powder room hand in hand.

THE SILENCE FILLING THE CAB IS A HEAVY ONE. DANTE AND I stare in opposite directions, each looking out at the night sky as the coach makes its way back to my hotel. He managed to find us an unattended back door to escape the theater from without having to walk past the reporters again. But ever since we made it to my cab, Dante won't look at me. Maybe that's for the best. I don't know what I'd do if I saw regret in his eyes.

Then again, shouldn't he regret what we did? Better yet...shouldn't I? My reputation hit an all-time low, even before we were caught by Mrs. Vance. Now she'll do whatever it takes to make our moment of indiscretion public. At least she didn't drag a photographer along with her.

Even though I know I should feel at least a little regret over my behavior, I can't regret our kiss. It warmed my soul in a way I haven't felt in a long time, if ever. No matter how our moment of intimacy ended, it felt good being lost in it. Swept up by it. Consumed by passion.

Lust. Romance. They will always be your ruin.

Anxiety flickers inside me, but it melts away beneath the memory of Dante's lips on mine, of his palm curved over my breast.

No, I can't regret our kiss, only that Mrs. Vance spoiled it with her intrusion. How much different would this cab ride be if our kiss had run its natural course without any interruption? Would we have left the play in a far less agitated state? Would we be kissing now? The thought sends heat between my thighs, but my fantasy is spoiled when I look over at Dante's tense form, at the stiff angle of his neck as he stares out the window.

Indeed, I'd much rather feel that heated spark of passion than the uncomfortable energy that ripples between us now.

The cab rolls to a stop. We've reached my hotel. My pulse quickens as I wait for Dante to say something, to bid me goodnight, to do...anything but stare pointedly away from me.

Several seconds pass.

Nothing.

My stomach sinks.

I clear my throat to steady my voice. "Well...good-night, then."

He turns his gaze to me so abruptly, I wonder if he forgot I was even in the cab with him. Shaking his head as if to clear it, he angles his body toward me. "Amelie, wait."

Relief loosens in my chest. I reach for him, wanting to close the distance between us.

"You won't see me again."

I freeze, my hand mere inches from him. Quickly, I pull it back and fold it in my lap. "What do you mean?"

His eyes are empty, expression wan. "Ever since I stepped foot in Faerwyvae, I've done nothing but make your life worse."

I frown, studying the sorrow etched into the lines of his face, unsure whether I should laugh or cry. "You're being a little dramatic, don't you think?"

"I promised I wouldn't hurt you," he says, a slight quaver to his voice. "I promised Albert wouldn't hurt you either, yet we both have."

"I don't know why you're reacting so badly." I try to keep my tone light, casual, but I don't believe my words enough to deliver them with conviction. "It was a kiss, and only Mrs. Vance saw. Even if she were to spread word about what we did, it's not like society can demand more from us than we're already going to give. The expected recourse after such a scandal is for the parties involved to marry. Which we're already doing."

He averts his gaze, jaw tight. "No, we aren't."

His words spear my heart. It isn't that I've forgotten Dante isn't my real fiancé. More that I've grown adept at not thinking about the fact that I'm supposed to marry a stranger instead of the man I've gotten to know. The thought sends my gut roiling. "No one knows you aren't the real prince."

"No, I'm not him. You're marrying the man I serve. The man I swore to protect. The man who...who became my friend." He runs a hand over his face, eyes unfocusing. "I kissed his fiancé. His future wife. If I'd only persuaded him to take his rightful place, none of this would have happened."

"Well, this is a first. I've never had someone so heartily regret kissing me." I meant to sound cajoling, but my bitterness is evident in every word.

He returns his gaze to mine. "I don't regret it. Not at all."

My heart flips. Again, I get the urge to reach for him. This time, I keep my hands fixed firmly in my lap. Despite his confession over not regretting our kiss, the way he says it is far from warm.

"That's the problem," he says. "I should regret it. I should never have let myself desire you. You were his from the start."

"I'm not *his*. I was never *his*, nor will I ever be. I am my own person, and he and I were never meant to be anything more than an allied front."

"I know." He releases a heavy sigh. "I know you say that, but look at us. Look at what happened."

He slowly lifts a hand toward my face and brushes a thumb along my jaw. It's an effort not to let my lashes flutter closed, not to lean into his touch.

"If it had been him and not me from the very beginning, then perhaps you and he would have been the ones to..."

It takes me a few moments to understand what he's left unsaid. When realization dawns, I bristle. Fury crawls from my heart, my throat, infusing my tone. "Are you suggesting I would have fallen in love with Albert in your place?"

His thumb goes still on my cheek, hanging on the word *love*. A word we haven't exchanged. A word that should be forbidden to us.

"I can't speak for your emotions," he says, "but I'm certain Albert would have fallen for you. How could he not? If he'd met you even once, he wouldn't have had room in his mind for Holly."

My hands form fists in my lap, and I wrench my face away from him, leaving his thumb grazing only air. "It's insulting that you think affection can simply bloom from proximity regardless of the parties involved. It's even more insulting that you...that you consider your own feelings for me so shallow that just anyone could pick them up like a discarded glove and wear it like their own."

Dante sucks in a breath, as sharp as if I'd slapped him. I wait for him to take it all back, to apologize, to repeat the far softer things he said to me in the powder room.

"I shouldn't have confessed my feelings," he whispers. My heart crumbles in reply. "I should have kept them hidden, as befitting my mission. Everything I've done since I met you at the Salty Satyr has been selfish. I could have persuaded Albert to join your engagement tour. I could have refused to attend in his place. It wasn't required of me. I could have fulfilled my mission by protecting him as a guard. All it took was a single word of

Albert's refusal for me to jump at the chance of getting to know you. After the attack in the alley, I told myself the threat to his life was real, that my service as his decoy on our dates was tantamount to his safety. But even then I knew the attack was probably a coincidence. I let my feelings sway me from duty, and in doing so, I've made things worse. I've robbed Albert of the chance to earn your affection, gave him too much freedom which resulted in him compromising your reputation. Then I publicly assaulted a reporter. Then...then our kiss—"

"Dante," I say, rounding on him with the full weight of my aggravation, "this isn't one-sided. You aren't the only one who engaged in...in what we have between us."

He shakes his head and opens the cab door. "I take full responsibility just the same."

I watch him exit the cab and belatedly follow in his wake. Panic compresses my insides as I find him several paces away, back facing me. He's just...just going to leave? I run after him, ignoring the startled expressions of the passersby who look my way. The city of Lumenas is famous for being busy well into the evening, which means the sidewalks are still crowded with tourists. I can't find it in me to care about being spotted running after a man. Once I reach him, I grab his elbow. "I'm not done talking about this."

He faces me and frames my face with his hands. Relief sends my knees buckling. My lips part, expecting him to brush his mouth against mine at any moment.

But he doesn't.

Instead, he studies my face with a furrowed brow, as if memorizing it. I don't dare move. Don't dare utter a word that will prompt him to take his hands off me.

Finally, he speaks. "He will love you, Amelie. He will love you just like—" He snaps his mouth shut, throat bobbing. His voice turns hard. Formal. "This is the last time we meet. I will seek reassignment after you and Albert are married. You won't see me again."

He turns on his heel, but I encircle his wrist with my fingers. My throat tightens, seared by desperation. "Dante, wait. Please."

"I can't keep my promise not to hurt you, Amelie." He refuses to look at me, his voice nearly swallowed by the noise of the crowd. "But I will protect you. Even if it's from myself."

Gently, he extricates his wrist from my fingers and weaves into the flow of foot traffic. I'm left gaping at the place he stood, my chest a hollow void. I expect pain to strike me, for agony to render me senseless, but I feel only empty.

For years, I thought I didn't have a heart to break. That I buried it along with the dead body of my first love, determined never to love again. Now I know I was wrong. My heart wasn't dead and buried. It was always here with me. Warming me. Teaching me to trust, to make friends again, to repair my relationship with my sister.

But now...

Now I fear I've lost it for good. For the man who holds it now is one I'll never see again.

19

Two days later, I can safely admit Dante was right; he has made my life worse. My name has returned to the scandal sheets, linked both to the story about my fiancé assaulting a reporter on the red carpet and the widespread rumors of my powder room kiss. Thankfully only the former comes with photographic evidence, although I've seen several hand-drawn renditions of me and the false prince locked in a vulgar embrace. I suppose it would be worse if word was spreading about Albert and Holly Abercrombie too, but not a hint of that scandal has been uttered. It seems Dante's threat to Eaton Farris was enough to silence him, not to mention all the work he did before the premiere to halt the story in its tracks.

My chest squeezes at the thought of Dante going through all that effort. For me.

I release a sigh, a sound that has filled my cottage like a melody on repeat for the last two days, and try to focus on my work. I've been fluttering about a pale blue gown for hours, sewing its final embellishments of silver buttons and seed pearls on the bodice, but my heart isn't in it. I can hardly look at the gown without my eyes straying to the one gracing the dress form in the corner of my living room—the dusty rose dress I wore to the premiere. I should have thrown it away for all the trouble it caused and for the bad memories it carries, not put it on display. I told myself I needed to check for stains and tears, but the truth is, I wanted to see it. To honor it, if only for a little while. The memories it carries are more than just bad ones. It holds good ones too. The kiss, of course. The sweet words Dante said beforehand. The way he looked at me when I walked down the stairs to the atrium.

Dante aside, the dress also reminds me of my incredulous discovery that the dragon silk lace adorning it catches aflame without burning the fabric beneath it or my skin. What a stunning display that would be, to showcase a dress covered in literal flame!

A flicker of excitement sparks within me, but I quickly tamp it down. Flaming gowns might excite my fae clientele, but they would never go well with the humans I'm currently trying to impress. Not that I have much hope of impressing them at all now. Bartleby's next showcase is five days away, and I haven't heard a word from them regarding my participation. With my reputation in tatters, I doubt my upcoming wedding to the prince will mend it.

I clench my teeth against the nausea that turns my stomach and thread my next seed pearl a little too aggressively. My needle comes through far harder than I anticipated and pricks the tip of my finger. I give a start at the sudden bite, but the wound heals before a bead of blood can even rise to the surface. Still, it's enough to force me to pause. I drop my needle, letting it dangle from the pale blue thread now hanging from the bust of the gown, and begin pacing the length of my living room.

Four days. That's how long I have until I marry a stranger. A stranger I'll be meeting tomorrow night.

That is, if I decide to go through with the final stop on my engagement tour—a ball held in my home court of Autumn. It seems so futile now. What could the real Albert and I do to counteract the damage done at the premiere? Sure, we could show everyone how in love we are, how prim and proper we can be in public without letting our passions get the better of us. Albert can prove he isn't the violent prince the scandal sheets are now saying he is.

Hope swells in my chest, but it's a hollow one. Even though I know this final tour stop could sway public opinion, it does nothing to alleviate my grim mood. Because everything inside me dreads meeting the real Albert.

My eyes flash to the letter lying open on my tea table, half buried beneath bolts of fabric. It arrived yesterday, bearing word from the prince that he would be attending the ball with me. I tried so hard to convince myself the letter was from Dante, that it was his way of telling me he'd changed his mind and would take Albert's place one last time. But I knew better. The handwriting was slightly off from the previous two letters I received in Albert's name, and as I read them in my mind, I could not reconcile the voice as Dante's. Which means I'll have to face the real Albert—my real fiancé—at the ball tomorrow.

And then marry him two days after.

My lungs constrict as anxiety crawls through me, raking invisible claws over my insides. It wasn't supposed to be this way. I was supposed to marry the prince with detached resolve. I was supposed to use Dante as a tool to improve my reputation, not...

Not fall for him.

Not open my heart only to lose it.

Now I must marry a man I do not love—a concept that once gave me comfort when Evie first proposed it but now feels like a vise crushing me from all sides.

Dread and rage battle within me, boiling into a roar that surges from my throat. With it comes a spark of flame lighting each palm.

I lift my hands and stare at the red fire, witnessing my frustration made tangible. Fueled by my growing anger, I march over to the dusty rose gown and punch the air before it, sending fistful after fistful of my fire to douse the dress. It takes less than a minute before I'm winded, but it feels good to have channeled my rage, to have utilized my fire instead of suppressing it like I always do.

Catching my breath, I step back from the gown. Surprise washes over me. Even after all the fire I threw at the dress, only the dragon silk lace burns. It seems to have drawn the fire like a magnet, once again leaving the other materials unscathed. Like before, the color of the flames has cooled to a pale gold. They flicker over every inch of the lace, from the hem to the layered flounces, bodice, and decorative rosettes. My rage calms, allowing me to extinguish the fire in my hands, leaving only awe in its wake.

The dress, with its warm and elegant flame, is more beautiful than I ever could have imagined.

A knock sounds at my door, startling me from my reprieve. I rush over to the gown and smother the flames with a quick brush of my hands over the lace. Then, collecting my composure, I make my way to my front entrance. Only when my fingers brush the handle do I recall I'm dressed in only a silk bathrobe. Getting dressed seemed like too much effort this morning since I wasn't planning on leaving the house. I consider running to fetch a shawl, but it's likely just the post.

Arriving with more news of scandal, I'm sure.

With a deep breath, I open the door with as much poise as I can muster in a bathrobe.

I pull my head back as I find my sister and Foxglove on the other side of the threshold.

Evie rushes to speak before I can. "Foxglove says you haven't been to the studio in two days."

"And we saw the papers," Foxglove adds with a grimace as he pushes the bridge of his spectacles.

I look from my sister to my friend, taking in their worried expressions, their eyes welling with sympathy. Part of me wants to dismiss their concern, to say I'm fine, and pretend my heart isn't aching. But...but maybe that's not what I need right now. Releasing my hold on my pride, I let a sad smile curl my lips and open the door wider for them.

"The good news is," Evie says as she lifts her hands to reveal two glass bottles, "we brought a lot of wine."

～

AN HOUR LATER, I'M SPRAWLED ON MY COUCH, CRUSHING half-finished dresses and probably staining them with a hefty dose of Agave Ignitus wine too. In my wine-addled state, I can't find it in me to care. Not after baring my wounds to Foxglove and Evie. Or as much of them as I'm willing to share.

I told them about Dante, confessed that he's the one I've been seen with all this time, and that I've neither met nor corresponded with the real prince. I even told them about our kiss, although I didn't go into much detail regarding what it did to my heart. From the pointed glance they exchanged, I suspect they know. Especially after my chin began to wobble beneath the weight of my suppressed sob when I described our bitter parting.

"So, they sent a spy into our midst during an act of peace," Evie says, narrowing her blue eyes from the other side of the couch. Her legs are thrown over mine, and her long auburn hair spills halfway from its updo.

Meanwhile, Foxglove lays on his side across my tea table, his head propped up by his fist. He takes a long swig of wine from the bottle, then passes it to Evie. With a dreamy sigh, he says, "I love it when a guy gets violent on his lover's behalf. Did you swoon, Amelie? Tell me you swooned."

I cradle the second bottle of wine to my chest—one I've kept to myself and have every intention of finishing off alone. "I didn't swoon," I say, my words too thick on my heavy tongue. "I was mad at him."

Evie takes a drink, then hands the bottle back to Foxglove. She arches her brow. "Mad because you thought he dallied with that actress."

I lift my head from the dress I've been using as a

pillow and cut her a glare. "I was only mad because he canceled our date and brought shame to our charade. He and Albert are free to dally with whomever they like, so long as it isn't done in the public eye." I say the last part too quickly, revealing the lie infused with my words.

Evie and Foxglove exchange another look, one that has them both smirking.

I sit up straighter and throw a ball of discarded silk at each of them. "I don't know what has the two of you so amused. It doesn't matter how I felt or what happened. I have to marry Prince Albert in three days, and he didn't even serve his purpose. Dante ruined my life."

Evie's expression turns more serious. "Did he though?"

"How can you ask that?"

She purses her lips before speaking. "It just...it seems, from the way you described spending time with the spy that you...dare I say enjoyed his company?"

"Or his tongue in your mouth," Foxglove mutters with a sly grin.

I scoff at them both but can't summon an argument. They'd just see through it anyway. So I seek a different truth. "Dante ruined my career."

Evie rolls her eyes. "He didn't ruin your career."

"He did. Bartleby's won't have me now. There's no way."

My sister opens her mouth but pauses, as if reconsidering what she wants to say. Leaning forward, she takes my hand in hers. "I know your career is important to you. I know you want to grow your label in the human market. But I think your heart is more important. Do you still want to go through with this? With the marriage?"

I blink a few times. Is getting out of the marriage even an option?

Evie nods, as if reading my unspoken question. "Now that we know they sent a spy to act in place of the prince, we have grounds to end the alliance without being blamed for it. King Grigory would have known sending a spy here could compromise the peace between us, and he did it anyway. If you want out, just say the word."

My mind goes empty. "What...what about the peace between our countries? Improved trade?"

She squeezes my hand. "The benefits of peace with Bretton are only worth the cost so long as it doesn't compromise your heart."

Tightness sears my throat at my sister's care. Is she truly willing to risk the alliance she and the Alpha Council forged just to protect my heart? And...do I want my heart protected? Do I want to admit I haven't given up on love after all?

I'm saved from coming up with a reply by another knock at the door. With a groan, I extricate myself from the couch, then cross my living room on unsteady legs. It seems I've had more wine than I realized.

A startling thought occurs to me as I reach the door, although I don't know why I would consider such a thing: *what if it's Dante?*

Why would it be Dante?

It couldn't be him!

It would never be him.

Despite my internal argument, hope flares in my chest, spurred by Evie's offer to end my unwanted marriage—

All pleasant fantasies fade as I find the female winged

fae standing on the other side of the door. It's the postal carrier. She hands me a letter and flies off, leaving me blinking at the return address.

It's from Bartleby's.

My mind seems to sober at once, and I tear open the letter with eager fingers. Evie and Foxglove rush over to me. With wide eyes, I read over the correspondence.

Dear Miss Amelie Fairfield,

We are pleased to welcome you back to Bartleby's. After much deliberation, we have decided to cut ties with Mrs. Maureen Vance and regret to confess we were acting under the impression that you were at fault for the scandal that erupted at the previous showcase. New evidence has proven the contrary, courtesy of several recent reports filed by other designers regarding Mr. Howard Vance's repeated improper and unwanted behavior. Bartleby's is a family company with strong values of propriety. While we agree that taking a man into a dressing room was poor form on your part, we acknowledge that Mr. Vance must be held accountable for his actions and assumptions. As for your latest scandal, Miss Fairfield, we are uneasy about your public displays of affection. However, we will be satisfied by the prompt wedding that will soon take place. Once you and Prince Albert are wed, you may resume participation in our show-cases. We look forward to seeing your work.

Sincerely,

Grace Marlowe

Showcase Director, Bartleby's

I stare at the letter, alternating between excitement and chagrin. While it bears the news I've been hoping for,

I can't help but feel indignant over the terms required for me to return to the showcase.

Once you and Prince Albert are wed...

Evie and Foxglove read the letter over my shoulder, making grunts of approval.

"Good," Evie says. "I'm glad the other women came forward. That wretched son-of-a-harpy deserves to be put in his place."

Suspicion crawls up my spine as I assess her words, the way she doesn't sound at all surprised. The way she says *the other women* as if she knows exactly who filed a complaint against Mr. Vance.

Slowly, I turn around to face my sister. "Did you do this, Evie? Did you make this happen?"

She pales but denies it with a curt, "No."

I open my mouth to bully a confession from her, but Foxglove speaks first.

"I did." He lifts his chin, meeting my gaze with defiance. "I looked into the matter and sought out the Vances' former designers. Turns out you weren't the only one Mr. Vance victimized, and I wasn't about to let that slide."

My mouth falls open as shock ripples through me. Foxglove did this? He got other women to file complaints against one of the most powerful men on the isle? As moved as I am by his care, disappointment quickly darkens my heart.

"You shouldn't have done that," I say, my voice barely above a whisper. "You know how important it is that I establish my career by my own merits—"

"Amelie Fairfield," Evie interjects, "when are you going to get it through your head that it's all right to be saved?"

The blood leaves my face at the ferocity in her tone.

She takes a step closer, hands on her hips. "It's all right to get help. With your life, with your career, with your heart. There isn't anything wrong with being saved."

As she says it, darkness pools deeper into my chest, echoing the last time I truly and fully let myself be *saved*. It was when I was engaged to King Aspen and desperately wanted Prince Cobalt. The man I lusted for promised to save me, to make everything perfect. And I believed him. Let him take charge. Let him *save me* from my unwanted pairing so he and I could be together. Then, in his final act, he stepped in front of a grenade meant for me. Died to save my life. Took his last breath after affirming he still loved me, even in the wake of the awful things he made me do.

On one hand, his first promise of salvation was a lie. On the other, his final act literally saved my life.

It's left me torn ever since, made me untrusting of aid and interference given for my highest good.

Evie must see my internal thoughts written on my face, for she takes my free hand in hers. "It's time to let go of your past, Ami. You're wiser now. You know the difference between love and lust, know that neither is something to be ashamed about. You also understand how to identify those you can trust. And I promise you, it's safe to let those people help you."

"What if I'm wrong?" My question comes out tremulous. "What if I trust the wrong person again?"

"You'll survive," she says, holding my gaze with fiery intensity. Then her mouth curls up. "And anyone who does you wrong, we'll kill."

While I know she's being sincere—in that morbid

way of hers—it invites a sense of levity into the room. "Promise?"

She nods. "Promise."

I read the letter once more.

Foxglove wrings his hands. "What will you do?"

"My offer remains," Evie says. "If you want out of the marriage, say the word."

My stomach ties itself in knots. In my hands lies the very thing I've wanted. The very thing I've been working toward for years. Taking my place at Bartleby's will prove I am worthy of the most esteemed human clientele. I only have to do one thing to make all my dreams come true.

End my scandal by marrying the prince.

"I know you want to honor your human heritage by claiming fame with the humans," Evie says. "But please remember Mother never wanted us to reject our fae sides. She only hid our bloodline to keep us safe. In all other things, our mother was rebelliously fae. And you can try all you want, Amelie, but you cannot separate your work from your fae nature. Your creativity comes from fire magic."

I say nothing because I still can't bring myself to admit my greatest source of motivation—to claim fame over something she has no hand in. While it would be so easy to simply be satisfied with my renown amongst the fae, I'd never be able to erase that I only got there because of Evie.

But what if she's right? What if there's nothing wrong with being saved?

For a moment, I allow myself to consider what it would be like if I no longer cared about my standing with the humans. If I no longer had to balance on the knife's edge of propriety. My chest immediately swells with relief.

But wouldn't that mean giving up on my dreams? Accepting failure and defeat?

Or would it be more like letting go of a burden?

I glance from the letter to the unfinished blue ball-gown, its bodice dangling a threaded needle. One ball. One meeting with a stranger. One marriage contract to be signed. Then I'll have everything I've wanted.

Plus a lifetime of playing pretend with a man I don't love.

"You don't have to answer now," Evie says.

I rouse myself from my tangled thoughts and force a lighthearted smile. "Good, because we still have wine to finish."

I toss the letter on my side table and return to the couch with my companions. We drink. We ignore further talk of serious topics. Yet, all the while, I steal glances at the dusty rose dress that entranced me with its gorgeous flames.

20

Meeting the real Prince Albert in person is much like being presented with what appears to be a designer gown, but upon further scrutiny, is a poorly constructed knockoff. It's ironic, of course, because the man sitting beside me in the backseat of the automobile is supposed to be the authentic version. Yet I can't look at him, can't so much as breathe the same air as him, without comparing him to Dante.

I glance over at the prince. My heart stutters at how similar he looks to Dante. It's clear now why the spy was recruited as the prince's decoy. While they certainly don't look like twins by any means, their similarities are uncanny. Both have sharp bone structures, blue eyes, and golden hair that falls haphazardly in the same roguish fashion. Their heights and lean builds are nearly identical.

I'm reminded of two young women who lived in Sableton—the town I grew up in. They too held such strong similarities that I couldn't help but confuse them. If they were ever in the same room or standing side by side, I could clearly decipher that they were different people, but should I encounter either of them alone, I couldn't help getting them confused. I got into the habit of evading any attempt at greeting either woman by name, should I be mistaken, and I later found out I wasn't the only one. Despite identifiable differences, they were simply two people who were constantly getting mistaken for the other.

I imagine the same phenomenon applies to Dante and the prince. A vague acquaintance could easily mistake them as the same person.

But to those close with either man...

My belly flips as I realize I now consider myself amongst that party. Someone close to Dante.

Intimately close.

Albert chuckles to himself, oblivious of my silent assessment. He sits as far from me as he can manage, sipping a flute of bubbly champagne with one hand and browsing the *Trundale Tattler* with the other. From how often he titters at his own name being mentioned in the scandal sheets, he must be getting a kick out of the drama Dante and I have stirred up. Although, I can't be certain that's how he feels, for the man has hardly said a word to me since he and his driver arrived at my cottage to pick me up in his automobile—the car Dante named Bertha, I recall with sentimental affection.

Albert didn't so much as offer me his hand in greeting, only held open the door and told me to be careful of Bertha's leather seats. Had this meeting occurred two weeks ago, I'd be pleased beyond belief. All I wanted then was a fiancé who kept his distance and provided zero risk to my heart. Now that my heart has been thoroughly captured by an unexpected thief, Albert's distance feels aggravating. Well, not his distance, exactly. More the fact that he isn't Dante. In letting my guard down with the spy, I've experienced what true closeness feels like. What safety feels like. Safety isn't distance like I thought it was. It isn't guardedness or lack of lust and attraction.

My gaze sweeps over the prince, assessing the way his leg is crossed away from me, how his attention is engrossed in his paper. If Dante were here, he'd tell the prince his body language is all wrong.

Albert's gaze darts from the *Trundale Tattler* to me, startling as if he'd forgotten my presence. "Pardon? Did you say something?"

I force myself not to wince at his voice. Even his tone is like Dante's, yet it's all wrong at the same time. It's not quite deep enough. Not quite warm enough.

Shaking my head, I avert my gaze to the window, watching moonlit autumn trees give way to city streets as we draw closer to the city of Oakenshire. Albert doesn't press me to say a word. There is something I must tell him before the night is through, but now is not the time.

First, we have a ball to attend.

THE BALL IS HELD AT THE OAKENSHIRE BALLROOM. IT'S A masked ball—a tame event, compared to the glamoured balls the fae are known to host—to raise funds for the city's new hospital. I don't need to check the timepiece tucked in my purse to know we're running late. Albert showed up thirty minutes after the time we agreed upon. Further evidence is demonstrated by the lack of people loitering inside the lobby of the ballroom, its vacancy visible beyond the large glass doors.

I shrug off the velvet cape I wore over my gown, not bothering to bring it inside. Then I retrieve my mask from my purse and tie it behind my head, careful not to disrupt my elegant chignon. My mask is a simple domino made from pink silk. It does its duty of complying with the expectations of a masked ball without distracting from my dress.

The driver, who I recognize as Mr. Digby, opens my door and helps me out of the backseat. Albert meets me on the sidewalk and offers me his arm. He too wears a mask—burnished copper with a slight beak over the nose—but it isn't enough to hide the widening of his eyes when he sees my dress for the first time, no longer hidden beneath my cape.

"You're showing a lot of skin." He doesn't elaborate whether that's a good thing or a bad thing, but his grimace says enough. The man may have a rakish reputation with women, but I take it he prefers his wife to present herself as demure.

"I am, aren't I?" I say dryly, unable to note that Dante's reaction would have been far different from Albert's. In fact, I already know exactly how Dante would have responded, as the dress I wear now is the very same I wore to the red-carpet premiere.

Well, if Albert disapproves of my gown now, I suppose he'll like it even less in a minute or so.

I take Albert's elbow and allow him to escort me inside. A pair of footmen greet us at the front doors and guide us to where we'll make our grand entrance. Anxiety squeezes my lungs as one of the footmen directs us to a circular landing above a short staircase that leads to the dance floor. A quadrille is underway, and those not dancing chat with their companions. Albert presents the Master of Ceremonies a card with our names while I take my chance to remove my gloves. Albert catches sight of my bare hands as I tuck my gloves into my purse.

"What are you doing?" he whispers. "You can't remove your gloves at a ball. It isn't proper. Or...or is that something you fae find appropriate?"

I give him a false smile and let my indignation grow to anger. It floods my chest and trickles down my arms, filling my palms. Where normally I resist the heat that begs to explode from my hands, this time I yield to it. Red flames fill my palms, and I bring them down to my skirt, releasing the fire to light a piece of lace trim.

The Master of Ceremonies leaps back, as does Albert.

The spark grows, catching the full length of the lace. The startled reactions of those on the landing draws the attention of the guests on the dance floor. Gasps erupt as the flames catch on more and more of my dress. Thanks to a quick alteration I made, thin threads of dragon silk extend from one row of lace to then next, then the next, allowing the fire to spread on its own until every inch of the special lace is aflame with a gently flickering golden blaze. I close my palms, and the flames in my hands go out.

The music stops, either from the song's natural conclusion or my blatant grab for attention. I meet the eyes of those who look up at me, finding everything from repulsion to awe. Lifting my chin, I meet their gazes without falter.

This is who I am, I silently convey, as much to myself as those who look at me. *I, Amelie Fairfield, am human and fae. Creative and violent. Sweet and dangerous. Accept me or don't, but this is the real me.*

It's a risk. My rebellious entrance could get me removed from the ballroom at once. More than that, my actions tonight will assure my second chance with Bartleby's is permanently revoked. But it's a risk I'm willing to take after my conversation with Evie. It made me realize gaining human approval won't make me human. It won't return the innocence I had before I fell in love with a cruel fae prince. Hardening my heart won't erase my past, and rejecting help from others won't guarantee my happiness. I'm starting to understand that my determination to do things alone has had an adverse impact on my joy.

Evie's words echo through my head, steadying me. *There isn't anything wrong with being saved.*

Dante's words join hers: *You may not need saving, but you are worthy of it nonetheless.*

"Good Almighty, Miss Fairfield," Albert hisses. "Are you out of your mind?"

I ignore him and quirk a brow at the Master of Ceremonies. When I recall how much of my expression is hidden behind my domino mask, I gesture an impatient hand at him.

The man shakes his head, face pale beneath his black half-mask, and addresses the ballroom. "Prince Albert of Bretton and Miss Amelie Fairfield."

Albert flinches as I take his arm, but thankfully he doesn't shake me off. Instead, he trembles a little as he escorts me down the stairs. It seems in all of Dante's efforts to impersonate the prince, he failed to fully portray his cowardice.

Once we reach the bottom of the stairs, the music begins again. While some continue to gape at my flaming dress, most have the decency to look away and feign indifference.

Albert adjusts his tie, then his mask, as if he wishes to be free of both. "I think I liked it better when my dear friend Dante was in the spotlight," he says under his breath, a note of panic in his voice. "People don't look at me in quite the same way here as they do back home. I think you might have upset someone. Did you really need to make such a spectacle?"

I glance down at my gown as if I can't fathom his concern. "Has no one told you I'm a fashion designer? Making a statement is expected of me."

"Fashion designer, yes. Scary fae creature, no. From the way Dante spoke about you, I expected you to be civil."

A sad smile twists my lips at his mention of Dante. While I doubt I was always *civil* with the spy, especially during our first encounter, it warms my heart to think he spoke highly of me. Then again, Dante was likely playing matchmaker, in part. He expected Albert to be capable of falling in love with me.

He will love you, Amelie. He will love you just like—
Oh, how wrong he was.

"Shall we dance?" I ask since he hasn't.

His eyes fall to the flames illuminating the lace at my neckline. His mask fails to hide his cringe. "Will...will I get burned?"

"No, the flames are harmless," I say, weaving my still-bare fingers through the gentle blaze. "Merely warm." When his expression remains hesitant, I retrieve my gloves from my purse and put them back on.

It satisfies him enough to say, "Very well."

We take our place with the other dancers and start into a waltz. His grip is limp, both at the middle of my back and beneath my hand. The other pairs keep their distance, and the couple next to us looks at my gown with outright hostility.

"Good Almighty, I need a drink," Albert mutters, not bothering to hide his eagerness for our dance to end.

I suppose I share his feelings, which means it's time to say what I must.

"Your Highness, there's something I must tell you."

He glances at me before hastily looking away. "Dante told me about the kiss, and I already know about your scandal. Oh, and your ground rules. I am fully aware of what our arrangement means, so fret not. I neither expect nor want more from you."

Yet another string of words that would have sounded like music to my ears had we met weeks ago. Steeling my nerves, I make my confession. "Albert, I...I regret to inform you, but...I cannot marry you."

His eyes go wide behind his mask. "Pardon?"

"I cannot in good conscience go through with our marriage arrangement."

He stops in place, and a pair of dancers nearly collides with us. For several seconds, he does nothing but stare at me. I expect anger, or at least an act of wounded pride. So I'm quite surprised when he opens his mouth...and laughs.

He halts the sound with his fist, but it doesn't hide his mirth. "Oh, thank the Almighty, Miss Fairfield. You couldn't have delivered better news."

I'm torn between a smile and a frown. "You aren't upset?"

"Upset?" He scoffs. "No, I'm not upset. I couldn't be more relieved. I never wanted—" His mouth snaps shut. "Wait, no. This is all wrong. I can't go home. My father... you do understand he'll kill me, right? This marriage was meant to be my punishment for wrecking his favorite automobile last fall. If he considers me responsible for destroying peace with Faerwyvae..." He closes his eyes as a troubled look crosses his face.

"I'm sorry, Your Highness," I say, but my words are lost on him. With a vacant expression, he wanders away from me, muttering to himself. He disappears into the crowd. In his absence, I wish I'd followed after him. Not to try and speak with him, but to avoid the scandalized stares that lock onto me now. Those nearby whisper behind gloves and silk fans. Several assess me with unabashed sneers.

The prince and I kept our voices low enough so as not to carry over the music, but to witnesses, it's obvious our dance ended in some sort of falling out.

I release a heavy sigh. It doesn't matter. This is what I came here to do. To tell the truth about what I do and don't want. To show society who I really am and be unashamed of what they see.

Now that I've done what I came to do, I feel...good. Not great but good. That's a start.

I turn on my heel, ready to exit the ballroom with my

head held high, but a masked male figure stands in my way. He extends his hand.

My heart does a flip, sending my pulse hammering. The man who stands before me may hide his visage behind a full-face white-and-gold mask, and his suit may be inconspicuously plain, but I know who he is, even before he utters a word.

"Miss Fairfield." The sound of my name on his lips is as soothing as a kiss on the brow. "May I have the honor of finishing this dance?"

21

Dante takes the space Albert vacated with the ease of a missing puzzle piece locking into place. Where the prince's touch was loose and limp, Dante's is firm. Anchoring. Perhaps even claiming. One hand lifts mine, caressing it as I lay my palm over his, while the other rests low on my back. The steadying pressure paired with his too-welcome nearness makes me stifle a gasp. Albert may have kept his distance, but Dante closes inches like a moth to a flame. With us, it's the staying apart that feels difficult. And stay apart we must for—regardless of my rebellious statement with my fiery gown—we are at a formal ball.

"Ready?" Dante asks, and I hear the smile in his voice. It's criminal that I can't see his grin behind the full mask.

I give him a nod and we find our steps with ease, melding with the flow of the other dancers as if we've been swaying to the song all along.

"You're here," I say, finally finding my voice. "I...I didn't expect you to be. Why...why are you here?"

He leans closer as we step and sway. "I'm watching over Albert from a distance like I should have done from the start."

My disappointment at his answer is palpable. Despite my joy in seeing him, in being close to him once more, I'm reminded of how I felt when he left me after the premiere. A spike of anger sharpens my tongue. "Then why are you with me instead of watching him now?"

He doesn't answer right away. Instead, he holds my gaze as we shift and turn, in harmony with the other dancers moving across the floor. With our next turn, his eyes dart briefly away from me. "Albert is at the refreshments table downing a glass of wine while simultaneously flirting with a blonde who is...ah, unsurprisingly, it's Holly Abercrombie."

We turn again, and I try to catch sight of wherever he was looking. I see nothing beyond the other dancers and the chatting crowd. I suppose Dante is trained to notice things most others disregard.

"He must be happy to see Miss Abercrombie," I say stiffly.

His eyes flick sideways. "No, he's hiding now that he realizes it's her."

"Why is he hiding? I thought they were in love."

"She might be in love with him, but..." His gaze returns to mine, and my stomach flutters at the sudden weight in his stare. "I fear I've given my friend too much credit. I don't think he knows the meaning of love."

My throat constricts at the word. "Why are you here, Dante? With me, I mean."

He releases a sigh behind his mask. "I'm sorry I broke my promise. I know I said I'd stay away from you."

I want to tell him I'm not sorry, but I'm still too wounded. As much as I understand his reasons for having left me that night with a vow to stay away for good, it still hurts. "If you're so sorry, then why did you break your promise? I thought you never wanted to see me again."

"You know as well as I do that my actions had nothing to do with lack of want, Amelie."

He's right, and I can't keep my hackles up much longer. Already I feel my walls coming down, melting in his proximity like snow on a sunny day. "Then why? Why did you ask me for this dance?"

"I saw you standing alone, saw Albert walk away..."

I arch a brow. "And you wanted to rescue me?"

"Yes," he says without an ounce of shame. "I wanted to rescue you, so I came to offer you a dance. Though, people are still staring at you, so I think I've once again simply acted out of selfish desire."

"What selfish desire would that be?" Unable to help myself, I arch closer to him, discarding propriety until our chests are nearly touching.

"The desire to be close to you."

"You aren't afraid of my flames?"

He doesn't so much as look down at the flickering golden blaze that licks against his suit jacket, his trousers, everywhere our clothing touches. He simply trusts they aren't burning him.

"I could never be afraid of your fire," he says, each word pointed. Heavy. Carrying a deeper meaning hidden between the lines. But his next words leave no room for interpretation. "I missed you."

My heart thuds against my ribs, a tempo that

threatens to pull me out of synch with our waltz. Yet it's a far more tempting beat, one I don't think I want to ignore for a second longer. "I missed you too."

His hand slides lower down my back, the pads of his fingers tightening against my gown as if he's fighting not to pull me flush against him. "What happened between you and Albert just now?"

I swallow hard. "I told him I can't marry him."

He stumbles, catching himself before anyone but I could notice. "Why?"

The melody begins to slow, initiating the end of our dance. In a matter of seconds, it will be time for us to part, and I still have one more truth to tell.

"Because I don't love him," I rush to say. "And I...I know now that I deserve love. I don't want to live without it. Nor do I want to live without—"

Say it, I urge myself. *Tell him you want him to stay.*

But my words won't come. A darker part of me taunts that I should keep quiet. The last time I confessed feelings for someone, I became an accomplice in starting a war. Worse, I...I became consumed by violence. Revenge.

The song rings out with its final note, and the couples around us separate to dip into curtsies and bows. My pulse quickens with urgency. It's now or never.

We step apart like all the other couples, but Dante won't release my hand. "I accept you, Amelie, no matter what it is you want to say. So please say it."

I accept you. It's a simple phrase, but it means so much to me, more so as I stand before him in my bold gown. If he accepts me, then he accepts *all* of me. My human and fae sides. My fury and flame.

I can do this. I can say what lingers just behind my lips—

Someone taps me on the shoulder, and I nearly jump clear out of my skin. I expect it to be an inquiring dance partner, but when I whirl to the side, ready to bite off their head if they even try to ask me to dance, I find someone unexpected—not to mention unwelcome.

Mrs. Vance meets my gaze with narrowed eyes. She wears a forest green ballgown with a matching velvet domino mask. "You and I should talk, Miss Fairfield. The two of us have unfinished business to discuss."

Dante takes a forbidding step toward the woman, his posture rigid. I place a hand on his chest, halting him in place. "No, Dante," I whisper. "I'll speak to her."

I certainly don't want to talk to the woman, but if today is a day for truth telling, then perhaps Mrs. Vance deserves an honest explanation too. Not for her husband's actions, but for my own. I won't apologize, but I can explain my perspective when I took her husband into a dressing room.

Ignoring my companion completely, Mrs. Vance says, "Meet me on the south terrace next to the gardens." Without waiting for my reply, she turns on her heel and disappears into the crowd.

Dante scowls after the woman. "You're certain you want to be alone with her?"

"I'll be fine. But first, there's something I need to tell—"

"Albert," Dante mutters, spine going straight as his eyes sweep the room. "Damn it, where did he go?"

My heart sinks. Of course the prince has Dante's full

attention. It probably won't even matter what I say to him. His loyalty lies not with me.

I force a smile. "Go ahead and find him. I'll be all right. Thank you for the dance."

I don't wait to hear his reply or see how quickly he darts after his charge. Instead, I head across the ballroom toward the south terrace, dread weighing down my feet while unspoken confessions poison my tongue.

MAUREEN VANCE STANDS WITH HER BACK FACING ME AT THE far end of the terrace, where the paved marble stones give way to tall garden shrubs cloaked in shadows and moonlight. The walking paths beyond the shrubs appear empty, as most guests are indoors enjoying the dances and company of others.

At the sound of my footsteps, Mrs. Vance turns to face me. She looks me up and down with clear distaste. "Are you going to make me look at those ridiculous flames?"

I give her an overly pleasant grin. "Yes."

She huffs a mirthless laugh. "Then let us make this short. Miss Fairfield, I want you to end your engagement to Prince Albert."

I pull my head back, perplexed by her words. Of all the topics I expected her to have brought me out here for, my arranged marriage wasn't one of them. While I could admit my engagement has been already severed, it's none of her damn business.

Removing my mask, I meet her eyes with the full heat of my indignation. "Why would you make such a demand? Are you against peace between Faerwyvae and Bretton?"

"No, that's not it at all."

"Because your request sounds an awful lot like treason."

Maureen pales. Then, with an indignant scoff, she rifles around in her green silk purse and retrieves an envelope. I tense as she closes the distance between us, but she only flourishes the envelope's contents. It's a photograph. "I think you'll reconsider when I show you this."

My eyes widen at the black-and-white depiction of a couple locked in a heated kiss. Their faces are shown in profile, revealing the unmistakable visages of Albert and Holly. How in the bloody oak and ivy did she get that?

Keeping my voice as level as I can, I say, "How kind of you to be so concerned for my heart, but I assure you, it is at no risk."

She lowers the photograph, lips curling into a hateful grin. "Because your engagement is a sham, isn't it? I've known from the start, Miss Fairfield. You aren't the lovelorn couple you pretend to be. You may be fooling others, but you aren't fooling me."

I raise my hands in mock surrender. "You've caught me."

"End your engagement or I'll release these photographs to the public, and everyone else will know the truth. They'll realize you only entered this engagement to escape your scandal with my husband."

"Release them then," I say with a shrug. "Are we done?"

She stammers, mouth flapping before she manages a

coherent word. "You...you think you're above the judgment of society? You think your reputation can survive
where mine could not?"

"What is this really about, Maureen? Why are you so
determined that I remain unwed?"

She takes a step closer, venom lacing her tone. "I want
you to experience at least a taste of the ruin you've
brought upon me."

"What ruin? Your name wasn't the one bandied about
in the scandal sheets."

"Perhaps not, but do you think I came out of it
unscathed? Have you any idea what your actions have
caused? No, because you're nothing but a selfish harlot.
Bartleby's banned me from every one of their department
stores, all because I told them I'd withdraw my support if
they continued a working relationship with you. I had to
beg for my invitation to tonight's ball. Beg! My name has
been sullied. Did you never stop to think about me?"

I feel only a flash of pity in the midst of my raging ire.
"Mrs. Vance, I regret taking your husband into that
dressing room, but my motives were only to do my job. It
was a mistake in judgment on my part, and for that, I
apologize, but nothing else was my doing."

"You brought Howard's indiscretions into the public
eye."

"If we are to blame everyone but your husband, then
why not bring Lydia Mangrove and Eaton Farris into the
fray, hmm?"

"I do blame them. And I blame my husband too."

I throw my hands in the air. "Then why aren't you
taking this up with him?"

"I did. I told him how I felt about his hurtful behavior,

about his blatant disregard for the rules of our marriage, and do you know what he did? He served me with divorce papers. Our marriage is over. He'll get the whole of Vance Industries—a company I helped build. All because he can break the rules while I can't. And if I can't, you shouldn't be able to either."

My pity grows, extinguishing some of my rage. It isn't enough to excuse her behavior, but it does make me see myself in her. Her talk of marital rules reveals a glimpse at a future that could have been mine. She has the very thing I thought I wanted—a loveless marriage. If I hadn't called off my engagement to the prince and proceeded with our nuptials with a cold heart, I could be where she is now.

Mrs. Vance shakes her head. "I should have known better than to expect more of you. You think you're above the rules, coming here with your vulgar gown, ordering your fiancé to violently defend your honor, kissing him in public. You think you can do whatever you like and not pay the price. I'm willing to teach you a lesson by force. Boys."

She says the last word a little too loudly, and the shrubs at the end of the terrace begin to rustle. My heart leaps into my throat as two large men emerge from the shadows.

22

I take a step back, but before I can reach the door, a third man strides onto the terrace behind me to block my exit. The three figures watch me carefully but don't attack. Not yet, at least. The way they shift side to side, fingers curled into fists, knees slightly bent as if ready to spring into action, tells me they are more than capable of violence. A shiver runs up my spine at the terrifying awareness that we are completely and utterly alone. The garden paths are empty. I passed not a single soul in the dimly lit hall leading here.

She chose our location well.

Maureen's lips curl at the corners.

Rage sparks in my chest, running down my arms at once. Heat laces my palms, a prelude to the flames that beg to ignite. "What do you want from me?"

"They'll be holding you for ransom until your engagement is called off."

I bark a laugh. "My engagement is already over, you daft harpy. Did you not miss the quarrel the prince and I had on the dance floor? You've won. I will not be marrying Prince Albert. Are you satisfied?"

"I don't believe you."

"It's true. I'm sure you'll see it in the papers in a matter of days, if not tomorrow. If you'd prefer an answer now, by all means, go have a chat with my former fiancé."

Her nostrils flare beneath the curve of her mask. "No, I will teach you humility, Miss Fairfield. You must learn your place. You can't be allowed to break rules without being punished like the rest of us. If you refuse to suffer the consequences for your social missteps, then you'll suffer a few days tied to a chair until your sister comes to save you."

I grit my teeth and unleash the heat in my palms. Red flames coat my hands, burning yet another pair of gloves to ash. I shift my stance, placing all three men in my periphery.

The men leap back, as does Mrs. Vance. She can't hide her shock. "Miss Fairfield! What are you—"

"You didn't tell us she was fae," the first man hisses. "The Durrely Boys don't mess with the fae. This isn't what we agreed to."

The Durrely Boys.

The gang that attacked me and Dante...

Now I notice the brass pin each man wears on their collar, the very same emblem Dante pointed out after he turned our alleyway assailants into corpses.

"I paid you to do a job," Mrs. Vance says, backing away several more paces, eyes locked on my hands. "You already messed it up once."

I blink at her. "You...you orchestrated the attack in Jasper?"

She lifts her chin. "It wasn't supposed to be an attack, merely a...a fright. Your cowardly prince was supposed to tuck his tail between his legs and sail home on the next ship."

My mind reels. The attack wasn't a coincidence after all. But instead of Albert being targeted by someone who sought to prevent peace, I'd been the mark all along.

She shifts her gaze to the three men, giving them a pointed look. "That so-called cowardly prince ended the lives of your comrades. Take her already!"

Only one of the men sneers at me, but the other two maintain wary expressions. None attempt to close in.

The first man repeats, "We don't mess with the fae. It's the only way the Durrely Boys can operate without getting shut down."

"Oh, I'll shut you down," Maureen says through her teeth. "I'll put an end to the Kolville job. You think I don't know all the details? If you're so afraid of the fae, I'll inform the authorities about the job and ruin the Durrely Boys and Vance Industries in one fell swoop."

"The Kolville job," one of the men whispers. "Our biggest haul of the year."

Maureen's expression turns smug. "Yes, and if you want to keep your *big haul* and the money I already paid you—not to mention whatever ransom you decide to charge her sister—then you'll do as you agreed."

"Is her sister fae too?" one of the men mutters but receives no answer.

I could tell him she is, in fact, fae. If he learned of her identity, he'd wet himself. The three of them would run into the night at the mere mention of Evelyn Fairfield. But as much as I've slowly begun to accept letting my sister's renown aid me, it isn't pride that keeps me silent.

It's vengeance.

An old friend I haven't met in decades. A dark companion I buried alongside lust, love, and trust. But in freeing the latter, I've freed the former.

Vengeance, rage, passion, lust.

All born from the same element.

Fire.

"If you won't hold her for ransom, then at least make her hurt." The cold cruelty in Maureen's voice cuts like an iron blade.

"We can make her hurt," one of the men says, tone resolute.

"Good." Mrs. Vance steps off the terrace, making her cowardly retreat as the men close in around me.

I hold my position, letting my anger grow. Letting my rage fuel my flames until they burn hot enough to coat my skin in a sheen of sweat.

The first man charges for me, fist aimed at my midsection.

I splay my hand over his face and encase his flesh with fire.

The man leaps back, crying out as my flames scorch his skin. I whirl to the next man, finding him gaping, eyes bulging as they dart from my palms to his companion now cradling his ruined face. Clenching my jaw, I dart toward him, but something drops from above and falls onto the terrace floor.

It's a man.

No, not just a man, but...Dante.

His mask is gone, but he now holds his cane.

Although *hold* isn't the right word for how he swings it into one assailant's legs, then cracks it against the skull of the other. The first man goes tumbling forward while the other presses a hand to his temple and stumbles off the terrace. The burned man follows, trailing agonized grunts. The final attacker tries to flee as well, but Dante slams his cane into the back of his knees and catches him from behind in a chokehold. Soon the man goes limp in the spy's arms.

I glance from where Dante stands now to where I saw him drop down from. A narrow outcropping lines the wall above, several feet beneath an empty balcony. "You descended a wall and dropped from the side of the building. Is that something you do?"

"When I must," he says, chest heaving. Not from being winded, I realize, but from...fear. Or anger, perhaps. Dante releases the unconscious man, letting him drop unceremoniously to the terrace floor. "I used restraint this time. He's not dead."

His statement has me torn between amusement, terror, and shock. We just fought violent members of a gang, and I...I helped. More than helped. I burned a man's face.

I wait for guilt to creep in.

But it doesn't.

This is who I am. Fury and flame.

Dante closes the distance between us. I extinguish my flames, leaving only the harmless blazing lace of my gown. His voice turns strangled. "I never should have let you meet with her alone."

"I was obviously able to take care of myself." I keep my tone light, but my words have his expression falling.

He purses his lips, one hand tightening around the head of his cane while the other opens and closes at his side. Then, with a deep breath, he takes a step back. "You're right. You...you don't need me to rescue you. This isn't my place, I'm—"

I mirror his steps, reclaiming the inches he put between us. A warm smile curves my lips. "Thank you, Dante. For coming to my rescue even though I can save myself."

His eyes widen with surprise. He holds my gaze for several long beats before he seems to recall the situation we're in. "I should tie him up." He gestures toward the unconscious assailant. "I heard some of what was said. We must bring him to the authorities at once. He can confess—"

"Dante." His name leaps off my lips, my confession desperate to be heard before I can swallow it down again. "I need to tell you something."

He reaches for me, but he doesn't take my hand. Instead, he pauses, letting his palm hang halfway between us, his arms quivering with restraint. Whether it's out of respect for me or because he truly doesn't want me, I know not. All I know is that I have to tell him what's been hiding in my heart.

I relieve his hesitation and take his hand in mine, giving it a deliberate squeeze. "I want you to stay."

He says nothing, his entire body going still.

I'm starting to lose my nerve, so I blurt out the rest before I can think better of it. "I know you're loyal to Albert and to Bretton, but—"

"Loyalties can change," Dante says, stepping closer. Dropping his cane, he grasps my other hand. "Just like hearts can. My loyalties have already shifted, Amelie, right beneath my feet. I came here to protect Albert and I ended up protecting you instead, even as I made things so much worse for you."

Tears prick my eyes. "You didn't make things worse. You made things better. So much better."

"Your reputation—"

"To hell with my reputation. I already have everything I need. Friends. Family. A flourishing career with the fae. The only thing missing..." I nibble my lip to keep it from trembling. "Will you stay, Dante? Even if Albert goes back to Bretton, will you remain...with me?"

He releases my hands and frames my cheeks between his palms. "I couldn't have brought myself to leave, even if you hadn't asked. I'm yours, Amelie. Completely yours."

He presses his lips to mine, his kiss fierce with desperate need. I meet that need with my own, wrapping my arms behind his back and pressing him hard against me. Warmth floods my chest. Not the fiery heat of rage or even the molten core of lust and passion. This warmth is more like the golden flames embellishing my dress. Soft. Gentle. Nurturing. My heart seems to expand along with it, creating doors, windows, wide open spaces where once there were only walls.

We kiss until we're out of breath, until reality sinks in, reminding me of our comatose audience of one. The assailant may be asleep now, but if Dante was correct about the restraint he used, the man will soon wake.

As if reading my mind, Dante pulls away just far enough to cast a glance at the figure's slumped form. Satisfied with the lack of impending danger, he lets his forehead rest against mine. "How will we make it work?

What will happen to the peace between our countries? Will we destroy everything because of..."

He doesn't need to finish. I know what he's trying to convey.

Will we destroy everything because of our love?

It casts a haunting shadow over me, an echo from the past. I already caused destruction because of love before. Can I really risk doing so again?

The dark side of me teases and taunts, reminding me that love comes at a cost. It destroys. It hurts. It kills.

But no. That's all wrong. Love doesn't destroy. It heals. The dark thing I once shared with Prince Cobalt all those years ago wasn't love. It may have been lust, perhaps, but not love. What he felt for me wasn't even love, no matter what he wanted to call it. It was obsession. Possession. He may have saved me, sacrificing his life for mine, and he may have whispered love with his last breath. That doesn't mean his actions define *love*.

I may not be ready to say that word out loud just yet, but I'm eager to learn its true definition. What it means to me. To *us*.

First, I must find a way to make *us* possible.

And I already have an inkling of how to make it so.

I place my hand behind Dante's neck, stroking the hair at his nape. My heart hammers as I prepare to state my next words aloud. Panic threatens to render me mute, but as I hold his gaze and sink into the comfort of his blue irises, I know my question will fall into safe hands. A safe heart.

"Dante, Spy of Bretton, No Last Name, will you marry me?"

He inhales a sharp breath. For one terrifying moment,

I fear I was wrong. That he'll pull away, say no, say I'm crazy. Or at the very least, demand an explanation for such an absurd proposal.

Then the warmest smile I've ever had the privilege to witness stretches across his lips, deepening his dimples in a way that makes my stomach flip. "Yes, Amelie Fairfield, I'll marry you."

We come together in a gentle press of our lips, a tender promise.

When he pulls away, mischief sparkles in his eyes. "However, I expect a damn nice ring."

I bark a laugh. "I'll get you a ring, darling."

He shakes his head with an exaggerated sigh. "You didn't even get down on one knee."

"We'll save that for our honeymoon," I say with a wink. "And I'll be on both knees."

He blinks at me, registering my bold flirtation. He pulls his bottom lip between his teeth, and his voice dips into a low purr. "Don't you dare presume you'll be getting on your knees for me before I've had a chance to worship every inch of you first."

Heat stirs deep in my core. I part my lips, eager for another taste of him, when the sound of movement has us leaping apart.

We turn toward the no-longer-unconscious man as he struggles to push off from the ground. Dante gives me an apologetic look. "It seems we still have work to do. Or I do, at least. This bastard has a date with the authorities and a confession to make."

The man scrambles to his feet, swaying slightly. "I'll tell them nothing."

Dante keeps his eyes on mine, flexing his fingers in preparation for a fight. "We'll see about that."

I lift my chin and let my inner fire course down my arms until a blaze of red heat fills my palms. "I'll be right beside you, dearest."

Dante doesn't argue. Doesn't tell me to stay back and let him do what he's been trained to do. Instead, he gives me an approving nod. Together, we charge toward the man. His eyes widen as soon as he sees my flames. Dante retrieves his cane from the ground, making the man cringe back.

I already know it will be too easy. He'll be begging to make a confession before we lay so much as a hand on him.

Good.

He should fear us.

Alone, Dante and I are frightful enough. But together...

The Durrely Boys, Vance Industries, Lydia Mangrove, Bartleby's—however many enemies or disapproving sources try to block our path, none will stand a chance.

But we do. I know we do.

We'll show them all.

EPILOGUE

ONE MONTH LATER

The first time I fell in love, I started a war. I gave my power away, trusted the wrong man, and vowed to scorn love forever. Good thing I'm not a pureblood fae and can lie, for today, in breaking one vow, I take another.

Dante and I stand before a stone pedestal, hands clasped as a human priest from the Church of Bretton officiates our wedding ceremony with his opening remarks. Aside from the traditional priest, everything else about our wedding is unconventional. At least by human standards.

My dress isn't a puffy white gown but an emerald green spider silk dress in the fae fashion, with a deep neckline and gauzy skirt. Dante wears casual black pants, an open waistcoat, and a linen shirt free of tie or cravat, his sleeves rolled up to his elbows. In lieu of church walls lined with stained glass windows, we stand in a birch tree grove. The sunlight shining through the canopy of red-gold leaves above us casts glittering light upon the plush forest floor. Instead of a pipe organ, our wedding march is birdsong. Our only attendants are my sister, King Aspen, Foxglove, and Breeda. The latter flits over our heads, humming a tune that stands in contrast with the priest's monotone. It's hard not to laugh, especially when Breeda gets bored of fluttering and decides to perch upon the man's shoulder, making his face go pale as death. He doesn't miss a beat, though, and simply pretends the fire sprite isn't there.

Dante squeezes my hand. As I glance over at him, I find he too is struggling to keep a stoic expression. Despite how he purses his lips, his eyes are crinkled at the corners.

Something slow and warm like melted honey moves through me, a feeling I've come to call love. I've felt it more and more over the past month. Not that I doubted my feelings when I proposed to Dante. Still, this journey of the heart is a new one for me, and it helps to be reminded over and over that it's a path I do indeed want to travel. A path I *deserve* to travel.

"Marriage is a sacred union," the priest says, and I remember I'm supposed to be paying attention to him. A challenge, considering his dull delivery, expressing none of the passion I feel.

While I'd rather have a less somber figure overseeing our nuptials, utilizing a human priest from Bretton's church was one of King Grigory's demands. It was victory enough when my sister and the Alpha Council got him to agree to our new terms for a peace pact. None of us were willing to push it much further. The situation was tense when we first confronted the king about sending a spy into our midst and allowing him to act as a decoy when the point of the alliance was to establish trust.

It required some deception on our part. Not to mention asking my sister for help. Evie had to exaggerate her anger over being duped by a spy without swaying the Alpha Council toward drastic measures. Instead, the solution was a simple one: we would demand both the prince *and* the spy as our hostages. The prince would be given comfortable accommodations to live in Faerwyvae from now on, but since the spy was guilty of insulting the fae by taking the prince's place and testing for threats, he would be forced to marry a fae bride—me, of course, thanks to Evie's cunning.

Everything has strangely come full circle. Twenty-two years ago, I was given as a forced bride to a stranger. I rebelled against my arranged marriage and chose a different groom. I let that groom rescue me. Lied to my sister. Pushed everyone I loved away.

I've once again rebelled against my arranged marriage and chose a different groom. And again, I let my beloved rescue me. A few times now. This time, though, I kept my power. I let my sister rescue me too. Told her the truth. Brought everyone I loved closer to me.

I never would have thought experiencing an echo of my dark past could feel so healing. So much like forgiveness.

But it does.

The priest guides us into the part where we say *I do*. Then it's time to exchange vows. My pulse kicks up with eager anticipation as we face each other, hands clasped. This is the part of the ceremony I've been looking forward to, regardless of our monotone officiant, because I get to speak from the heart. We may be required to state traditional time-honored words—per King Grigory's demands—but that doesn't mean I can't pour that honey-warm feeling into each one.

Dante seems to be of the same mind. The priest delivers words for Dante to repeat back, and when he does, his tone is brimming with sincere conviction. Each promise to love and care for me through all stages of life is paired with a smile. He places my ring over the tip of my finger. It's a rose gold band designed to look like a twining tree branch that curves around my finger in a three-tiered spiral. Three dainty emeralds rest on each tier. He caresses his thumb over the back of my hand as he settles the ring in place.

Breeda flutters off the priest's shoulder to hover over my hand. "Oooh, that's pretty."

She's right, but I can't take my eyes off Dante to look at her or the ring. When I recall our vows someday in the future, I want to remember the sparkling warmth in his eyes, the beauty of his glowing smile, the potent love written over every inch of his face.

Evie whispers for Breeda to leave us alone, and the sprite obediently glides over to her.

Now it's my turn to deliver my vows. My lower lip begins to wobble as I encircle Dante's finger with his ring. It's slightly thicker than mine with only one tier and the same twig-like design. I repeat the priest's words, my voice far more tremulous than Dante's, due to the happy tears constricting my throat.

"I now pronounce you husband and wife," the priest

says, sending a trill of delight through my chest. "You may kiss the bride."

Dante doesn't hesitate to pull me against him and press an enthusiastic kiss to my lips. I wrap my arms around his neck, meeting his enthusiasm with my own. When we don't immediately draw apart, the priest clears his throat. Our guests, on the other hand, aren't put off by our lingering affection at all. In fact, they downright ignore it, encircling us with warm hugs or firm pats—the latter courtesy of King Aspen, I can only assume.

Once we finally manage to separate, Aspen claps Dante on the back. "Welcome to the family, Mr. Fairfield."

My heart swells at the sound of Dante's new surname. He was overcome with emotion when I suggested he take mine.

"Thank you, Your Majesty." Dante's eyes flick briefly to Aspen's intimidatingly large antlers, but he maintains a wide grin. The two have interacted only a few times over the past month, and Dante is still getting to know the fae aspects of his new home. So far, he's integrating rather well, if I say so myself.

Evie wraps her arms around my waist from behind and rests her chin on my shoulder. "Congratulations, Ami. I'm happy for you."

Foxglove barrels into me from the front, hugging us both. "So am I."

I manage to wheeze a laugh despite how tightly they're squeezing me. "I'm happy for me too."

Breeda circles over my head. "I knew I was witnessing a love story in the making. Remember when I said that? Hmmm?"

I catch sight of Dante grinning over at me. "I suppose you were right all along."

Foxglove and Evie finally let me go, but as soon as Foxglove steps back, I catch him wringing his hands, lips pulled into a grimace. When he sees me looking, he halts and hides his hands behind his back.

I narrow my eyes. "Foxglove..."

He releases a heavy sigh. "I hate to break up the buoyant mood so soon, but I suppose this is a good time to tell you...well...the press is outside your cottage right now."

My mouth falls open. "What? How did they..."

Dante and I exchange a knowing glance.

"Damn it, Albert," Dante mutters under his breath. "He had one job."

I roll my eyes. We should have known better than to rely on Albert to draw attention away from our real wedding location. King Grigory may have had his share of demands regarding our nuptials, but I had conditions of my own. The primary one being a small outdoor ceremony in the Autumn Court woods close to home. No guests, only four witnesses. To divert the press from guessing our real wedding location, we spread a rumor of a large ceremony at a posh hotel in the Lunar Court. Albert was tasked with being seen coming in and out of the hotel with various pieces of evidence in tow—a wedding dress, a florist accompanied by an assortment of bouquets, and an overlarge cake.

Foxglove resumes wringing his hands. "He performed dutifully until around noon today, when I got word that Holly Abercrombie had found him. He abandoned his post at the hotel after that and is now holed up at a gentlemen's club."

"It's all right," Evie says with exaggerated enthusiasm. "You can stay at Maplehearth Palace tonight."

"The press is there too," Foxglove says.

Evie scoffs. "Well...then I'll banish them. It's my palace. I'll set them all on fire if I must."

"Oh, yes," Breeda says, nodding her tiny head. "Do set them on fire. I'll help."

"No one's setting anyone on fire," I say firmly, although I can't keep my shoulders from sinking. All I wanted was a quiet night alone with Dante. No servants. No fanfare. No crowded hotels or busy palaces.

Aspen brings his hand to his chin in contemplation. "What about the manor?"

Evie frowns, but realization sparks in her eyes. "Yes! Aedylvine Manor!"

"Aedylvine Manor," I echo. "The mansion you gifted Prince Albert?"

"*Tried* to gift," Evie corrects. "And that was only if he married you. In our new agreement, he insisted on a townhouse in Port Dellaray. Which means the manor technically belongs to you. Or it could if I move the deed around." At my grimace, she rushes to add, "I know you don't want a manor. You're perfectly content at your cottage. But...you could have a summer home, couldn't you? The press doesn't know about it yet. Unfortunately, all the furnishings have been covered, and there's no staff—"

"Say no more." I look over at Dante, who nods. "We'll take it."

AEDYLVINE MANOR IS NESTLED IN THE AUTUMN COURT countryside north of Maplehearth Palace. It's some distance away, which means Albert and I have a short journey before we can finally relax as a married couple. Instead of hiring a cab, Dante insists on driving Bertha, which he somehow convinced Albert to let him keep.

As much as I disliked the vehicle at first, I don't mind it at all right now. Dante and I sit side by side in the front seat, watching the sun set over the sprawling crimson hills surrounding the quiet road. Soon I find myself entranced by the scenery. No matter how many years I've lived in the Autumn Court, I don't think I'll ever get over its beauty.

"Stunning," Dante says. I look over at him, finding his eyes on me.

"Me or the view?"

"You are the only view that matters," he says with a crooked grin. "But I can see the allure of the landscape. It's lovely here. Prettier than any fall season back in Bretton."

I search his tone for notes of longing, for any sign that he misses the home he left behind. But there is none.

"If the scenery puts that smile on your face," I say, reaching out to brush my fingers against his cheek, "then I suppose I can forgive Albert for failing at his job as a decoy today."

Dante shakes his head, mirth dancing in his eyes. "We should have known better."

"We really should have," I say with far less amusement.

"He's not so bad," Dante rushes to say, casting me a worried look. "You'll like him better when you get to know him."

I wrinkle my nose. "Must I?"

"He may be an idiot—perhaps the biggest idiot I've ever known—but he's still my friend."

"A friend you tricked into giving you his beloved car."

"He was foolish enough to assume I was only marrying you out of duty. He all but begged me to take Bertha in exchange for my great sacrifice. I might as well take advantage before he learns how much I—" His mouth snaps shut, and it takes him a moment to try again. "How much I *adore* you."

My smile falters. He was about to say *love* but stopped himself. Why? Because I haven't said it yet? Or...because his feelings haven't quite grown that far? I know where mine have grown.

"Do you regret it?" he asks, tone suddenly wary. "I keep waiting for you to regret it. To regret me."

I sit up straighter. "Why would I?"

He gives me a sad smile. "You gave up a prince to marry a spy. A spy who's currently unemployed until the Alpha Council decides if they'll give me a job. Albert, on the other hand, will always be a royal, no matter where he lives. No matter what he does. Compared to him... well, I'm just..."

My heart sinks at the vulnerability that crosses his face. I recall what he said about Holly Abercrombie. That he was, for a time, romantically involved with her. Before she chose Albert. I wonder if that wasn't the first time a woman has gotten close to Dante only to fall for his friend.

"You gave up part of your career too," he adds.

I angle my body to face him. "Dante, I didn't give up part of my career. I simply...let go of something I no longer needed."

Soon after my engagement to Albert was publicly severed, followed by the shocking news that I was going to be marrying the prince's decoy, Bartleby's revoked their invitation back to the showcase. I felt only a pinch of disappointment, but it was quickly replaced with relief.

"Besides," I say, "don't forget an *unemployed spy* took down a gang and opium operation."

Dante chuckles. "We did that together, darling."

He's right, and it fills me with no small amount of pride. It was almost effortless to get the man we captured to confess to the authorities about what Mrs. Vance had tried to do to me. With that, plus what I overheard about the Kolville job, a group of fae operatives—plus Dante— were able to bust a long-standing opium trade fronted by Vance Industries. Howard and Maureen are currently behind bars, along with the Durrely Boys who were present during the bust. Those who escaped legal punishment have successfully attracted the unwanted attention of the fae royals. They're on thin ice now. If they want to continue doing...well, whatever seedy activities gangs like to do, then they'll need to keep their actions in the realm of morally-gray-yet-legal.

"We make a good team, Dante."

"We do," he says, but there's something restrained in his tone, his posture.

I scoot closer to him. Careful not to steal too much of his attention from the road, I gently place my hand on his thigh. "I chose you, Dante. We're more than a team. More than political allies. I asked you to marry me, not just as a solution to maintain peace with Bretton but because... because I love you."

He whips his gaze toward mine, eyes wide. "You love me?"

"Eyes on the road." When he obeys, I add, "And yes, I do love you."

"Damn it, Amelie," he mutters, voice like a growl. I fear I said the wrong thing. That he wasn't ready to hear that word. "I wish I wasn't driving right now. Do you have any idea how badly I want to kiss you? How badly I've wanted to tell you I love you?"

His eyes find mine again, and I see hunger in them. Passion. Desire.

It emboldens me, sending a roiling heat deep in my belly. "I told you automobiles are nothing but trouble," I whisper, tone sultry. I tighten my grip on his thigh, stroking the tips of my fingers along his inseam. "If we were sitting in the back of a coach, we could be doing all sorts of things. Things we couldn't do in here, with or without a driver at the wheel."

The car swivels so suddenly, I stifle a shout of alarm. But Dante hasn't lost control of the vehicle. Instead, he pulls it onto the grassy shoulder beside the road. He turns the key, silencing the rumbling purr of the automobile. Then, holding my gaze, he says, "Come here."

The intensity in his eyes, his tone, has me aware of just how alone we are. There's no one else in the car with us, hardly another soul on the quiet country road. And we're heading to an empty manor, just the two of us. An unexpected timidity comes over me as images of what commonly occurs on one's wedding night fill my mind.

We've spent a lot of time together over the past month, going on dates, getting to know more about each other, taking our relationship public. But in terms of intimacy, we've yet to move past heated kisses. Dante wanted to take things slow with me, especially after I told him the full truth of my past. The hurts I sustained from Prince Cobalt's abuse. I've been ready for physical intimacy for weeks now, but the thought of being with someone in that way—someone I love—has my heart racing with the most delightful terror. I swallow hard and try to keep my voice level. "Why did you pull over?"

In answer, he encircles my waist and pulls me into his lap. "If you think there's any obstacle that can keep me away from you, you're wrong. I'll kiss you anywhere. Make love to you anywhere. Coach, automobile, closet, stable. Anywhere, Amelie."

His words send sparks of invisible flame over every inch of my body. I could laugh it off. I could giggle and pretend he's teasing me, but I know he isn't. And I don't want to take his words in jest. Not with the bright warmth flooding my chest, the heat pooling at the apex of my thighs. Wrapping my arms behind his neck, I lift my thin skirt and shift my legs until I'm straddling his hips. Only an inch of room remains between my back and the steering wheel, but I like how close the confined space forces us to be. "Show me."

His lips quirk into a devious grin. "Show you what?"

"Show me what kinds of things we can do in an automobile."

"Oh, Amelie Fairfield of little faith. I'll show you, my love. My wife. My fiery fae creature. Today and every day after this, I'll show you. I'll show you *everything*."

"Today and every day?" I echo. "That's a tall order."

He slides his hands up my back. One hand weaves through my hair while the other cups my backside. I roll my hips, and he bites his lip. "An order I'm more than happy to fulfill."

"All right," I say, voice breathy. Lowering my lips to his, I whisper against his mouth. "Let's start with right now."

NOT READY TO LEAVE FAERWYVAE?

Keep the magic alive! If you're craving another standalone fantasy romance, you'll want to read the *Entangled with Fae* series! Each book in this series is a standalone new adult fairytale retelling with a happily ever after guaranteee. They can be read in any order, but if you start with *Curse of the Wolf King,* you'll get a glimpse at Amelie two years before the events in *Married by Scandal*.

You can also take a trip to Amelie's past with *The Fair Isle Trilogy*, which takes place twenty-two years before *Married by Scandal*. See where Amelie first learned to turn her back on love in this epic romantasy series based around her sister, Evelyn Fairfield.

WANT MORE ARRANGED MARRIAGES AND FAE?

Arranged Marriages of the Fae is a multi-author series of short novels written by seven romantic fantasy authors on the same theme. These books can be read on their own, but you'll have so much more fun if you read the whole series:

- *Married by Wind* - Angela J. Ford
- *Married by Fate* - Jenny Hickman
- *Married by Scandal* - Tessonja Odette
- *Married by War* - Sarah K. L. Wilson
- *Married by Treachery* - Barbara Kloss
- *Married by Starfall* - Meg Cowley
- *Married by Dusk* - Brianne Wik

Find them all at:
http://www.arrangedmarriagesofthefae.com

ALSO BY TESSONJA ODETTE

ENTANGLED WITH FAE - FAE ROMANCE

Curse of the Wolf King: A Beauty and the Beast Retelling

Heart of the Raven Prince: A Cinderella Retelling

Kiss of the Selkie: A Little Mermaid Retelling

— And more —

THE FAIR ISLE TRILOGY - FAE FANTASY

To Carve a Fae Heart

To Wear a Fae Crown

To Spark a Fae War

PROPHECY OF THE FORGOTTEN FAE - EPIC FANTASY

A Throne of Shadows

A Cage of Crystal

A Fate of Flame

YA DYSTOPIAN PSYCHOLOGICAL THRILLER

Twisting Minds

ABOUT THE AUTHOR

Tessonja Odette is a fantasy author living in Seattle with her family, her pets, and ample amounts of chocolate. When she isn't writing, she's watching cat videos, petting dogs, having dance parties in the kitchen with her daughter, or pursuing her many creative hobbies. Read more about Tessonja at www.tessonjaodette.com

instagram.com/tessonja

facebook.com/tessonjaodette

tiktok.com/@tessonja

twitter.com/tessonjaodette